An Unobstructed View

An Unobstructed View

Jenness Clark

AS YOU LIKE IT

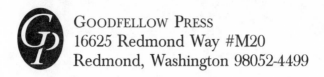

GOODFELLOW PRESS
16625 Redmond Way #M20
Redmond, Washington 98052-4499

(AS YOU LIKE IT) Redmond, Washington

ISBN: 1-891761-02-1
Library of Congress Catalog Card #: 98-074116

Edited by Pamela R. Goodfellow
Cover and interior illustration by Jenifer I. Rees
Cover photography by Jeff Pruett
Book and cover design by Magrit Baurecht

Printed on recycled paper in Canada

This is a work of fiction. The events
described are imaginary; the characters
and entities are entirely fictitious and
are not intended to represent actual
living persons or existing entities.

FOR
JOHN, ANNIE, AND WILL.

SPECIAL THANKS
TO MARIA
*$W.am
7/4

y God, Helen, how could you?" Margaret stood looking at the decomposed mass in front of her, its limbs stretched upward as if it were reaching out in a vain plea to save itself. "And once such a vision of loveliness," she murmured. Her sister Helen had started to slip in the past year, no doubt about it. Normally Helen would have attempted to cover up something so grotesque out of embarrassment alone. This time she had really gone too far. What if someone had seen it? Margaret glanced up towards the street in time to see her neighbor Colleen driving by in her new BMW, but the carcass was on the ground and safely out of sight. Of course now it would be up to Margaret to dispose of it. It was just like Helen to leave her messes for her sister to clean up only his time she'll hear about it, Margaret decided assertively.

She began to wonder how long this horrible thing had been here; how long since she'd been out in the yard for any length of time. It had been raining for six weeks, since the first of June, which was plenty of time for rot to set in. Maybe if she chopped off the limbs, she could stuff it into one of those extra-large leaf bags they sell at the hardware store and the garbage men would haul it off.

As Margaret turned to go up the front steps to the garage, she was startled by her neighbor Randal Weeks as he came around the curve of the steps. Margaret reddened and with out thinking, reached up to straighten her hair. She became more embarrassed as she recalled the haphazard ponytail she had thrown together this morning. Had she even brushed her hair at all? She tried to remember. Her eyes took in Randal's plaid shorts and matching pastel colored polo shirt. His clean-cut look certainly contrasted with her soiled gardening clothes. His shoes even looked polished. She wondered vaguely if people still polish their tennis shoes.

"Ye gods, what a horrid sight!" He almost knocked her over as he jumped back from the decayed remains. "What is it?"

Margaret grimaced. Just her luck to be caught by Randal, of all people. Although his wife was one of her closest friends, he was not one of her favorites. He could be so priggish and always had an opinion on everything.

"Oh, it's just a dead rhododendron bush." She tried to sound casual as she snipped at some leaves on a nearby Japanese maple.

"But it's full grown. How can it be dead with all the leaves still on?" He looked at her accusingly.

"And what is that goo oozing out of it? What on earth happened? What is going on?"

"Well, it's not as if you could see it from the street," she snapped in defense. The rhododendron was pretty horrible, but this was a bit much; he was absolutely shouting. She realized too late that she had just whacked the top off the poor little Japanese maple.

"What is that black sticky stuff?" He reached as if he were about to touch it, but immediately drew back with a little hop. A ladybug had landed on the crease of his shorts. He carefully leaned down, studied it for a second, and then gave it a hard flick into the air. "No sign of a stain," he said more to himself than to Margaret as he closely examined the fabric. That settled, he turned his attention back to the rhododendron bush, straining his neck as he took a closer look. Then his voice went into a higher pitch. "It must be some rare disease. I hope it isn't contagious."

"No, no, nothing like that." Margaret felt the need to reassure him even though she was a little irritated by now. "Helen was trying out some new kind of fungicide solution that she painted on the branches. It's a shame really. The yellow ones are so uncommon and it was Mother's favorite rhody. The bush was hanging on pretty well until Helen decided to go to work on it."

"It's just awful." He took another little jump backwards as the front door opened and Helen's heavy footsteps could be heard shuffling on the stairs. Their fine, brick Tudor house was below street level and was reached by walking down some stone steps. At the sound, Randal, who was at the top of the steps, turned and quickly hurried away back up towards the street. "Renee wanted me to remind you to come at 6:30," he called back over his shoulder.

"Should I bring anything?" Margaret shouted, but there was no answer. He was already down the street. Oh well, she could always bring a bottle of wine or maybe she would have time to check the roses, there might be some in bloom. Renee would love a nice bouquet.

"He was certainly in a hurry." Helen set down her new plastic gardening bucket next to Margaret. It was sparkling clean, complete with mesh pockets for spades and pruning shears. Margaret noticed Helen's makeup was heavier than usual and she was wearing a new shade of mauve eye shadow that added years to her looks. She suddenly looked well over forty. But then again, her face was all wrinkled up since she was scowling down at the mess in front of them. "Oh, this damn rhododendron bush! I'm glad it's dead. It's always been such a strain. God knows I did everything I could to save it."

"Well, there's nothing left to do but to dispose of it. Give me a hand, Helen, and we'll bag it up for the garbage man." Margaret quickly gave up on the idea of reprimanding Helen. She knew trying to reason with her was hopeless when she took on one of her defensive attitudes. Better to just get the thing into the garbage.

"But, Margaret, you know I had my heart set on working in the roses today. I've done more than my share of work on that rhododendron. Now it's your turn. I don't know why Mother ever planted it there." Helen continued to mutter to herself as she made her way up the steps to the street where the roses were. Margaret's shoulders sank in resignation as she was left alone with the sticky plant. Helen had always been a master at rationalizing things to suit herself.

This is much better, Helen thought when she reached the top of the steps and turned to look up and down the street. Up here she had a better view of the neighbors and the tip of Mount Rainier was just visible in the distance. There weren't many people out working today, which was a surprise, since it had been raining for six weeks and this was a Saturday, too. Only old Mrs. Applegate across the street was doing some weeding; nothing was ever new with her and Helen certainly didn't want to hear about the moss problem on her roof again. Mrs. Applegate looked up smiling, but Helen felt she had turned away quickly enough to avoid speaking to her.

Helen grimaced as she looked over the twenty wet and sickly rose bushes that covered the hill between the house and the street. Since it was only early July, not many had started to bloom yet. None of this concerned her for long, however, as she continued onto her favorite spot, the very edge of the roses next to the laurel hedge. Here there was a small hole in the hedge where, if she stood on her toes and leaned just a little forward, she could see clearly into her neighbor David's yard, all the way up to and including his house. The faint unsteady light of a TV glowed through the window. It was not a good sign.

"See, what did I tell you, he hasn't gone to work for three days and the PI is still on his front porch!" Helen shouted down to Margaret as she gawked through the hedge.

"But today's Saturday," Margaret murmured an answer that Helen could barely hear.

"Stop all the hacking and speak up. He won't hear you." Helen's voice bellowed past the roses and down the stairs. She glanced over to Mrs. Applegate and caught her peering across her lattice fence. Her yappy little dog was running back and forth in the yard. "I think it's happened. Don't you think we should do something?"

"Do something?" Margaret looked up. "But he looks healthy enough. I saw him yesterday. He's even let his hair grow a bit, and he's shaved off that nice trim beard he used to have. Look at all that pruning he did."

Helen looked grudgingly at the six garbage cans lined up neatly in front of his house. All of them were full of yard debris, clearly four hours of work there. When had he done all that? Maybe he had taken a good turn, a little burst of energy that he would pay dearly for later. He probably needed her help more than ever after all that work.

"We could take him a casserole, that chicken and rice one with the wine sauce. And in a nice dish, of course, so he would know we weren't worried about germs." Helen casually sniped at a rose bush, but she didn't bother to pick up the debris and put it into her bucket.

"But his mother hasn't come yet. Remember how she came three years ago when he had the flu? It could be that he's just on vacation. Give it a few weeks and see how he's doing."

"All right, Margaret. You can be so optimistic and irritating." Helen did not care for her sister's attitude. She was always looking on the good side and didn't know anything about David anyway. Helen was the one who had gotten to know him so well over the last few years. She was the one who really understood him. Never mind that at thirty-six he was almost five years younger. It wasn't that kind of relationship anyway. Things were just so comfortable: chats across the fence and a few dinners now and then, which Margaret usually cooked. And there was never any concern of his finding anyone else. Helen had long since decided he was gay and would never break her heart in that way. Of course there was the fear of his getting AIDS, but Helen had developed a plan of covered dishes and baked goods if that happened. She imagined herself nursing him quietly at his bedside until the end came, but her thoughts always stopped there. She couldn't imagine David gone. What would happen to her routine of keeping watch over his house, checking on his car, or monitoring his paper delivery boy? Sometimes she fantasized that a tragedy might bring them closer together, but she guiltily chased those ideas out of her head because after it was all over, what then? No. No need to think about any of that now. Everything was just fine as it was. It was just a nice cozy relationship that benefited all the parties involved. There was really no reason to worry about the future.

CHAPTER 11

By the time Margaret was finished with the rhododendron, she was covered with the black tar-like substance that Helen had painted onto its branches. Soap didn't remove it from her arms even though she scrubbed them with a brush, and the pre-wash stain remover didn't work on her clothes. Her T-shirt and work gloves would probably have to be thrown away. Finally, she made some headway with fingernail polish remover, but by then it was noon and she was starving.

In the kitchen she started to make lunch for Helen and herself. As she took the lunch meat from the refrigerator, her thoughts returned to the rhododendron and she began to wonder why her mother had planted it there by the steps. It had been five years ago this month since Mother died, and as Helen had pointed out at the visitation, their mother had transplanted it to that odd location right before her death.

"It should have been a sign to us," Helen had said at the time, but no one could figure out what it could have been a sign of. The bush had started to go slowly downhill immediately. Last summer Helen had taken it upon herself to save it.

Right after their mother's death Margaret had decided to move back into her girlhood home to live with Helen. She did not miss all those dark and cramped one-bedroom apartments she had lived in during the ten year interval between college and her return to Lakeview. The last five years had slipped by easily with a beautiful house and yard, no mortgage or rent, a great neighborhood located in the city full of old friends, and even an old Mercedes in the driveway. All this had given her the opportunity to keep the job she loved so much, a part-time position cataloging the Northwest Coast basketry collection at the nearby Princess Angeline Museum. It was much more fun than the obscure historical societies where most of her other classmates from the anthropology department had ended up working.

Of course, the main drawback was that she had to live with Helen. She spread the mayonnaise on Helen's turkey sandwich a little thinner than she had for herself. Helen could do without the extra calories. Living with her certainly had its problems, like being covered with tar for one, but people imagined it to be much worse than it was. Everyone seemed to absolutely gush with sympathy when the subject came up, as if Margaret were some kind of martyr, but even that had its advantages. Anyway, Helen was all right most of time. Living with her was certainly never dull.

Their other sister Joan, the oldest of the three, had found and married the perfect man. Dr. William Philbrick, chief surgeon at Olympic View Hospital, was a man who enjoyed getting direction, as Joan would always say. Margaret could never understand how the Good Doctor made any decisions at work without Joan there to direct him, since he was completely unable to decide anything for himself at home. But it was just as well. Joan wouldn't have lasted with anyone else. She had certainly grown up to be a much more dominant person than she was as a child, Margaret thought as she cut the sandwiches into small triangles the way Helen liked them.

Trudging in from the yard, Helen took off her gloves and set down her still clean bucket. "You didn't make anything for Joan. Isn't she coming by for lunch?"

"She said she didn't want to eat with us. They have an auction tonight and, you know, she likes to eat right before they go out. I think it helps with the bidding." Margaret set the plate on the table and restrained herself from adding that Helen knew full well that Joan had never eaten lunch in her life unless she was at a luncheon.

"Yes, I'm sure it would; what a good idea. Auctions can be so horrible." As Helen made a face, Margaret's thoughts drifted back to the last church auction where Helen had gotten the item numbers confused and paid seven hundred dollars for a gift-wrapping demonstration instead of the one week trip for two to Hawaii she thought she had bought. Luckily Joan, who had chaired the auction that year, placed the item quietly back on

the block, but not before Helen had bragged to
Louise and Colleen that she had paid only seven
hundred dollars for a trip to Hawaii, including
airline tickets. Louise and Colleen had made a catty
remark to Helen about it only last Sunday at the
after-service coffee.

"Now, Helen, maybe we shouldn't bring up
Fred and Susan's divorce unless Joan does first,"
Margaret said sternly as they moved into the
dining room to eat. But she knew that Helen would
bring it up anyway. There was no use in trying to
get her to keep quiet about anything, and besides it
was hard not to ask about Fred who was Joan's
only child and heir to all three sisters.

He and Susan had been married for only two
years when trouble started to brew just around
Valentine's day. After Susan moved out, Fred
developed a habit of coming over and slumping
down in the wing chair in the living room. Helen
had gone into a state of uncontrollable nervous
agitation, her behavior becoming even more
irritating than usual to everyone but Fred who,
in his depression, simply ignored her.

"Have some beans and rice," Helen had coaxed
Fred one afternoon as he slouched in the chair in
the living room. "Remember how you use to love
it when you were little? We would all sing, 'Love
you once, love you twice, love you more than
beans and rice'."

Margaret had cringed as she listened to Helen
singing. That little ditty would only make him even
more depressed and of course he wouldn't be
hungry with a broken heart. But then Margaret had
watched, surprised, as Fred reluctantly smiled and

then picked up the spoon. He ate it with relish but after he had finished the bowl he began to slump once more.

Joan had always been good about sharing her son with Helen and Margaret, but at the time of Fred's divorce things changed. Joan had left Helen and Margaret out of the loop at first, and then suddenly Fred had turned back to them for comfort. Margaret didn't know how to react because nothing like this had ever happened in their family before. It was not the idea of divorce itself that threw everyone off. It was just that things weren't going along in their routine way. Everyone's roles had changed, and relating to Fred as an adult to a child wasn't working anymore.

Fred seemed to have grown up too fast and Margaret felt that, at least in part, she was to blame because she had encouraged him to get married. Now she felt guilty about it. Sure, he had expressed some feelings of doubt right before the wedding, but didn't everyone?

She always thought it was her duty, as an aunt, to encourage Fred to do anything he felt like doing: "Go for it!" seemed like a great attitude for an aunt to have. At least that was what she told him at the time.

But now when she looked back on things, she could see that the argument Fred and Susan had had the week before the wedding, when Susan suddenly decided they should just wear matching rented tuxedos, should have been a warning flag.

Fred had even asked her, "Tell me the truth, Aunt Margaret, am I making a mistake?" It broke her heart to remember that conversation and now she felt at a loss. Should she apologize and take all the blame for herself? But that seemed like a silly idea; she could imagine him staring blankly at her.

But beyond the problem of what to do for him lay a bigger question. What kind of aunt should she be in the future? What line should she take with him? It was as if they had a new relationship to forge, that of two adults instead of an aunt and a nephew. Now that he had all these grown up problems, they seemed to have become just two ordinary people plodding through life without definition or title. It was all very disheartening for her, and she didn't see any way to resolve things until he had recovered from this divorce.

Margaret took the last bite of her sandwich and looked at the remains of some stale chips still on her plate. She pushed her dish away and wondered if Helen would clean up the kitchen. After all that business with the rhododendron, it was the least she could do.

Glancing at her watch, Margaret remembered that Joan was due to be over soon. She hadn't been by much since Fred stopped coming. Sometimes when Fred was over, Joan and Bill would come around and stand in the dining room, whispering with Margaret and watching as Helen fluttered around with various comforts that Fred seemed to accept unconsciously.

Of course the doctor had never been able to offer solutions in a situation of any kind, but in this instance even Margaret and Joan were just as useless. Margaret felt as if she wasn't standing on firm ground with Fred; as if, for the first time in her life, she had become a hand wringer.

All of this waiting and watching had gone on for three months but then had abruptly stopped about six weeks ago when it started to rain. Fred hadn't been seen since then. A few hurried telephone calls were all the contact either his mother or his aunts had made with him in over a month. He sounded fine, but they were still without any explanations.

"Maybe Joan has some news, and she'll be able to tell us how things are going. There's no chance for a reconciliation now though. I'm sure of that." Margaret's hopeless tone was more to herself than to her sister.

"But we've never had any kind of explanation as to what happened with them. Was there some sort of fight? And why did she suddenly move out?" Helen asked bitterly as she looked outside where it was beginning to drizzle again. No chance of seeing David now. She took a bite from her sandwich. Oh well, she could work on her mother's epitaph after lunch, it was always a pleasant way to pass a rainy day.

Helen had decide two years ago that the flat stone that marked their mother's grave was lacking something compared to their father's taller, more prominent gravestone. So she had taken it upon herself, indeed as her first real family responsibility, to have a larger headstone installed with a suitable quotation. It would be easy to move the smaller plain stone to the foot of the grave.

Picking out the granite color and shape of the marker had also been easy; the stone would, of course, match their father's. But deciding on a quote for the headstone was not such an easy matter. Because of the size of the stone, the quotation would have to be fifteen words or less. Finding a suitable one had become a stimulating but endless pursuit for Helen. She had envisioned a morbid quotation from Poe, who was her favorite writer, but Margaret and Joan had quickly vetoed all her favorite quotes by him. After that disappointment, Helen had decided to start reading poetry in search of something worthy of her mother, yet suitable for a headstone. She didn't want anything too cheerful. She had already spent over a year looking and it was becoming a little tiresome since she didn't like poetry much at all.

Where were her notes anyway? She abruptly pushed her plate back and ran into the library.

"Margaret, have you seen my epitaph notes? Never mind, here they are." She didn't want to loose her notebook. She quickly flipped through the pages. It was comforting to see all the poems and poetry she had already eliminated; there couldn't be that much left. It was gruelling to read each sentence over and over in order to understand it.

Then if she found anything she liked, she felt obliged to read a little about the poet's life so she could find out what type of person they were. She did not want any wife beater's or philanderer's quotations on her mother's grave, that was for sure. She quickly ruled out Lord Byron for this reason alone, not that she had found anything really good by him anyway.

Then David had given her the book, *Bartlett's Familiar Quotations.* She started to panic as she looked around the library for it. All these old Indian boxes and baskets Margaret collected were always cluttering things up. Finally Helen vaguely remembered that she had accidentally knocked the book into the waste paper basket yesterday, or maybe Margaret had put it there.

"Margaret, I can't believe you put my quotation book in the trash." She carefully picked her Bartlett's up and moved back to the dining room table. It was so thoughtful of David to give her such a nice gift; what a great idea it was. It had touched her deeply. She had no idea such a book existed. She had quickly looked up death, soul, tombstone in the index, and any other related topic she could think of, but to her dismay nothing seemed to fit. Her mother's life had not been dramatic enough for anything by Thomas Gray or any of the other writers she had found.

After checking the index, she decided to read the entire book so she wouldn't miss anything. This was much more fun than reading poetry, and easier to understand. She had found many quotations that seemed useful in her own daily life and she was only up to 'D'. Sometimes, she even forgot what she was looking for and had to go back and reread several pages at a time. 'Perhaps something by Dante would do,' she thought as she pushed aside her plate to set up her work on the dining room table. He was listed next in the book and he must have been preoccupied with death, all that business with hell and an inferno.

CHAPTER III

*J*oan Philbrick pulled out of her driveway, list in hand. She was irritated to see her neighbor's gardener's truck parked practically in the middle of the street, and on a Saturday too. 'These workers should finish their business during the week,' she thought grimacing as she squeezed past a lawn mower he had unloaded even more carelessly than he had parked. Well, at least there weren't any contractors out remodeling homes today. Usually their trucks were on every street corner. They virtually took over the neighborhood on week days.

Turning the corner, she glanced down at the list that lay waiting on the seat next to her. It was an exceptionally good one. She had made it at three in the morning, absolutely the best time to organize one's thoughts. Nothing gave her more pleasure than organizing one of her lists, except perhaps crossing off the items. Over half the things listed had already been checked off, which was usually the case with one of Joan's lists since she always wrote down even trivial duties such as getting dressed or taking a shower.

The most enjoyable duty of the day was always the last thing listed, and today's would definitely be fun. She had just booked the oompah band for the Homeless Children's Guild's first Octoberfest which was to be held on October tenth and she needed to get a deposit check from Louise, the guild's treasurer. As president of the guild, it was such a relief for Joan to be able to think about something besides the guild's stupid art auction, which was scheduled for next month. It was much more fun to think of Loser Louise and her best friend, Catty Colleen, and how they would have an absolute fit at the thought of the guild's dressing up in lederhosen and eating knackwurst. Joan couldn't wait to see Louise's reaction.

Louise had suggested a fund-raiser of croquet and classical music in the park. 'How absurd. No fun at all,' Joan thought. Not that she hadn't grown up on croquet and ice tea herself, her mother being from Baton Rouge. Joan enunciated her mother's birthplace in her best French nasals as she pulled into the shopping village. The annual auction at the University Art Museum was enough stuffiness for one year. "But it's all water under the bridge now," she chuckled out loud, for Louise and Colleen had decided to take the train down to Portland to go shopping so they could save on sales tax and had missed the last guild meeting. In their absence, Joan easily convinced everyone how fun it would be to drink beer and dance all night.

"'We plan on just sleeping at Saks,'" Joan flawlessly mimicked Louise's sugary sweet voice. "'Joan, you should join us; they could really help you with your wardrobe.'"

"I can't believe she actually said that to me," she continued talking to herself as she pulled into a parking spot. "Maybe I would, Louise, but how could I possibly stand to be around you for two days?" One quick stop here for coffee and then she was due at her sisters'.

In the bakery, Joan grimaced when she saw the size of the coffee line. Weekends were always like this. It was such a waste of her time to be standing there doing nothing. She decided against balancing her checkbook. An easier task would be to arrange her grocery list according to the items' locations in the store, something that could save her fifteen minutes on a busy Saturday afternoon at the supermarket. As the line moved slowly forward, Joan made use of the pastry counter to get her work done.

She had almost made it to the front when she heard an unmistakable, voice calling out to her from the back of the bakery. It was Louise. Joan tried desperately to think how she could avoid her; she quickly calculated whether or not she should make a run for it without the coffee. But after thinking about it for a few seconds, she decided that she couldn't duck out because if she failed to mention the Octoberfest to Louise now, things could get very awkward later when she went by to collect the check for the band.

She could just hear how Louise would twist things around to the other guild members: 'I had just seen her at the bakery that morning. I wonder why she tried to hide it? She must have been embarrassed,' Joan imagined Louise saying to the other members. Then there was always the chance that Louise might hear about the fest from someone else, ruining Joan's little surprise. Still, it was better to test the water before she blurted it all out, better to wait.

"Louise! Tell me. How was your little shopping expedition?" Joan smiled and raised her eyebrows, confident she was hiding her repugnance for Louise.

"Just fab...u...lous." Louise hurried up to her, drawling out her words and closing her eyes as she spoke, a habit that had always irritated Joan.

"Did you find lots of things?" May as well let her get the bragging over with, Joan decided.

"Yes, I just spent a fortune. I feel guilty even buying a latté." She opened her eyes and giggled.

"And what about Colleen? How did she do?"

"Oh, Colleen. Well, you know Colleen; she's so provincial. Really, I don't think she understands Saks." Louise could never resist a chance to discuss her best friend. "She's so sweet though." The line moved forward, and Joan placed her order. "And I heard all about the little Octoberfest. I didn't know you liked beer so much, Joan. That must be from the Southern side of your family, beer drinking on the levee and all that sort of thing."

"But it's supposed to be so good for you, Louise. Haven't you heard about the latest study? But how could you, without a doctor in the family?" Joan gave her a sad, sympathetic smile. "Anyway, William brought it all home from the hospital just last week. It seems beer is even better for you than that wonderful boxed wine from California you like so much. It's just great for your heart, they say."

"Fascinating," Louise smiled. "But did you hear that we have to change the Octoberfest date? It's too bad but at least it'll still be in October."

Joan's attention was turned back to the counter: her coffees were finished and ready to go: two in a bag with masking tape over the holes in the plastic lids and the third one in her hand. As she double checked the tape, she tried to decide if she could get away with pretending she hadn't heard that last comment.

It wouldn't pay to discuss things with Louise having the upper hand. Loser Louise obviously knew something she didn't and Joan's blood pressure was rising at the thought of it. In a bold move, she turned around, fixed her eyes on the window in the back of the bakery, and called out, "Denise!" Then she hurriedly turned back to Louise. "I've been trying to get her for two days. I'll have to talk to you later."

"Okay. Give me a call tonight. I have a couple of things about the art auction, too. I think we need to work on some promotion, don't you?" Louise sing-songed in a high voice as she peered out the back window of the bakery, looking for Denise.

"I can't tonight. Don't forget, we have the auction. We can talk there." Joan knew full well she wouldn't see Louise at the auction that evening. Louise had never in her life been to the premier social event in the city, the Blanco Auction.

It didn't help Joan's state of mind, however, to get in the last word with Louise. All this volunteer work she did year after year was so tiring... sometimes it seemed as if it wasn't worth half the effort. There was always a good cause, but these little problems had a way of creeping into things. It was starting to get to her. How could they possibly move the date of the festival, and why on earth would they have to? There seemed to be no way to find out without asking Louise.

She tried to think who else she could she call. By the time she pulled up to her sisters' house, she was beside herself with anxiety and felt as if the whole momentum of her day had gone downhill.

"Damn it!" she cried as she got out of the car. The coffee bag had tumbled over in the back seat. But instead of wiping it up, she stood in the street and tried to imagine what Louise had meant when she said 'we.' Someone else must have been involved in her little manipulating game, and it wouldn't be just Colleen.

No, that was an official 'we'; Louise usually referred to herself and Colleen as 'I.' Unless the 'we' was just a trick and there was no conflict with the date at all. And that comment she made about the fest still being in October couldn't be true because everyone knew that she and the Doctor were scheduled to go to a conference at the end of the month. They wouldn't even be in town during the last two weeks of October, so that little bit was obviously another trick on Louise's part.

"Hello, Joan," a familiar voice called out to her from across the street.

"Oh, hello, Mrs. Applegate. How are you?"

"Just fine." But Mrs. Applegate looked confused as she strained her neck forward to peer into the back of Joan's car. Ignoring her, Joan opened up the trunk and took out a zip-lock bag containing a spray pump bottle and a cloth. Kneeling into the back seat of the car, she carefully sprayed the coffee stain with the solution.

Then taking the chamois cloth, she blotted the spot off the seat. Luckily, she always carried a leather-cleaning solution in the trunk. As she watched the brown stain disappear, Joan's mind started to clear and her determination against Louise increased with each blot of the cloth. Louise would not ruin things for her, she resolved.

"Lattés for everyone," Joan called out when Helen answered the door for her. "Take this bag, Helen, and don't drop it, it's hot. Hold it from the bottom."

Helen looked down at the torn, wet bag with distaste and wondered if she could call Margaret to the door and have her carry it in; but before she could decide, Joan shoved it into her hand.

"Now, Helen, don't say a word. I got you a tall, single, nonfat, decaf mocha with no foam, and if you don't like it, please, just drink it anyway. It's what you liked the last time I checked. I just can't keep up with the way you are always changing your coffee preferences around."

Helen flashed a quick glance towards Margaret. She had changed her coffee preferences and could not possibly drink another mocha, they were too sweet, anyway. Besides that, she was back on caffeine.

She leaned over to peek into the bag. "No doubt you got Margaret a double short."

"Oh, Helen, really. This is just what I need to send me over the edge. You don't know what I've been through with Louise."

"It's okay," Margaret reached for the bag. "I'll take the mocha. It'll be a nice dessert after lunch."

But Helen beat Margaret to the coffee. She wasted no time grabbing the double short as quickly as she could. Then she moved back into the kitchen so she could hide from Joan and drink it the way she always did, with the lid still on.

In the kitchen, Helen stood next to the dining room door listening. Something was obviously up. She drank her coffee and smiled gleefully as she heard Joan shouting from the living room.

"Louise has somehow sabotaged the whole Octoberfest. I should have known this would happen. I just saw her at the bakery, and she said in her catty little voice that we would have to 'change the date,'" she mimicked Louise. "The band probably doesn't have another free Saturday in October. You know Bill and I are going to that conference at month's end. They only got back from Portland last night. How could she have messed things up so fast?"

Helen took a last gulp of her coffee in the kitchen and rejoined her sisters. She usually avoided Joan when she was in one of her 'harassed states', as she called them, but the double dose of caffeine gave her an extra boost of self confidence. "Maybe another event was already scheduled for that night," Helen cocked her head back and forth and almost sang out the words boldly.

"Did you check everything on the calendar for that date?" Margaret sounded meek and paranoid.

It was just like her to be scared of Joan when she was mad. She had invariably been a coward all her life, and always the baby of the family. Helen gave Margaret a dirty look and shook her head.

"Of course I checked," Joan snapped. "There are no auctions that night, and even the Junior League holiday gift mart is the weekend before. It's just so aggravating. How can I find out what's going on without sounding like I don't know what's going on?"

Helen chuckled to herself. It was fun listening to Joan being questioned about her organizational skills and seeing her get so upset.

"Well, call Denise," Margaret suggested as she moved into the kitchen. Helen watched from the dining room as she poured her half-finished mocha down the drain and threw her cup away. "She'll know. Louise must have gone into the shop before she went to the bakery. She would have to brag about all the clothes she bought at Saks, and what better place to do it than at Denise's shop?"

"And she said she wants to talk to me about 'promoting the art auction,'" Joan mimicked Louise again. "She has her nerve. Nobody promotes events better than I do and she knows it!"

Helen smiled to herself again. This was exciting. Maybe she could use it as an excuse to go over to David's later. They could have a nice chat over a cup of tea; he would get a kick out of this mess.

CHAPTER IV

argaret took a deep breath and opened her closet door. Although she had four hours to go before leaving for dinner at Renee and Randal's and then, more importantly, the museum board's annual party, she felt that she might as well get it over with and figure out what she should wear. Of course she wasn't at all concerned about her clothes at dinner; it was the party that worried her. For the last week, she had been dreading this moment as much as she had been looking forward to going, and now she panicked at the thought that she would probably end up wanting to wear something that needed to be dry cleaned. The museum board party was one of her favorite events of the year. She had woken up excited at the prospect of going until she happened to glance over to her closet. How absurd she had been, worrying about her clothes all week and trying not to think about it. Now here she was standing in front of her closet trying to remember what was at the dry-cleaners.

Choosing what to wear was without a doubt one of the most stressful aspects of Margaret's life. In the last few years she had developed an identity crisis about what type of fashion look was right for her. She had given much thought to the fact that the people at work and her artist friends dressed in a Bohemian style she could never fully embrace. Although that style was chic and comfortable with all the neutral, black, and gray tones, she felt that if her clothes were too contemporary, it might cause a stir in her more conservative neighborhood. Even though the museum was only about two miles from her house, the boundaries between the University and Lakeview were strongly marked, not only naturally by the lake but figuratively by the people. Although both groups were educated and fairly well off, they had very separate images they wanted to portray. What was acceptable in one neighborhood was unacceptable in the other.

The women who lived in Lakeview seemed to fall into two camps when it came to fashion: those who wore old athletic-type clothes like leggings with baggy sweatshirts, and the ones who always looked very tailored with their silk blouses, suits, and nylons. Margaret envied the athletic types. They were all thin and seemed to have more money than the tailored women. But there was also something a little disturbing about 'that bunch' as her mother always called them. There were always rumors of infidelity circling around them and they didn't seem to have very high moral standards about life in general. People always assumed they gave lots of money to charity since they always got seated up in front at all the auctions, but they never seemed to actually bid on anything. Of course, those court-side seats at professional basketball games were expensive, but were they in a way thumbing their noses at everyone? Margaret wondered. It was as if they were saying 'I can live an immoral life, look like a slob, and still command the respect of the community.'

Although they were much more comfortable in their clothes, and it was actually cheaper to dress that way, Margaret felt it would be hypocritical of her to embrace the athletic look. She did not have the money they had nor any interest in professional sports, and she had never exercised in her life. People might think she was trying to social climb if she dressed like a slob.

The tailored look, on the other hand, was what she felt people expected of her. Her sister, Joan, fit comfortably into that category but with a bit of an urban angle instead of the usual country style that most of the less fortunate guild members embraced. Joan seemed to have an attitude against fitting in too well with anything though: She always refused to wear navy blue or red, the flagship colors of most of the other guild members.

On the other hand Louise, her sister's arch enemy, with her white and navy blue wardrobe, was the premier country-tailored dresser in the neighborhood. She even wore nylons with shorts. Margaret had resisted that style as well. It seemed too dreary for her somehow. The dry cleaning was expensive and she hated wearing nylons. Leafing though her closet once again, she tried to think if she would have to wear them tonight. Maybe she could wear pants with knee-highs.

Instead of the country-tailored look, Margaret had settled into comfortable cotton twill pants, trouser socks, and loafers, an occasional blazer thrown over a T-shirt or blouse. Sometimes she wore an interesting pin or some fun earrings. She had felt for years that this was a good compromise between the bohemian and the tailored looks, that is until Louise had recently commented on how cute and collegiate her clothes were. Margaret was horrified. It hadn't occurred to her that she could be dressing in a collegiate manner, but of course now that she thought about it, she had to agree that that was how she looked.

What was it Louise had said? 'And you had such a good time in college, didn't you Margaret?' She had made the comment in such a sad, sweet voice, as if to say it had all been downhill since then. Margaret told herself that was just like Louise. She invariably managed to find out your weakness and then go for your jugular. She was always asking Joan if she had made this jacket or that skirt even though everyone knew that Joan didn't sew any of her own clothes.

Margaret's gaze drifted away from her closet and out towards the lake. It's not as if I'm trying to hold onto my undergraduate days, is it? She tried to think. We didn't dress in cotton twills and polo shirts then, did we? She remembered all the walks across campus, the visits to art galleries and, of course, Edward. We wore blue jeans and midi skirts with romantic blouses. Just the 'in' thing now, but she could not imagine herself wearing clothes like that again, except for the jeans. Maybe it's that I've kept my wardrobe on the level of a nineteen

. . . remembering all the
walks across campus, the visits to art
galleries and, of course, Edward.

year old all these years. She looked back to her closet and pulled out her olive green linen pantsuit. Perhaps it would look a little more sophisticated if she wore a different blouse with it this time, like something without a collar. That's it, she decided, from now on she would try and go with a more sophisticated look. She should ask Denise for some tips, since after all she did own a clothing store.

Looking in the mirror, she admired her new shorter haircut. She had recently started combing back part of her bangs so they would pouf up a bit, giving it a more modern look. Her new lighter brown color looked good too, better than the mousy brown that used to be her real hair color.

She leaned into the mirror to look more closely at her skin and smiled. That was her only problem, she decided. If she could just keep from smiling, there wouldn't be a wrinkle in her face. She should try to do a better job of smiling down instead of up, a tip she had picked up from a woman's magazine, but she never seemed to be able to remember to do that. It did have a slightly phony look to it, she decided as she smiled and pushed the corners of her month down on each side. It wasn't like a real smile. She would just have to remember not to smile so much.

CHAPTER V

fter an early dinner with Renee and Randal, Margaret walked back to her own house and got into the car without going in to check on Helen. She would be wholly engrossed in her Saturday-night video, something Helen looked forward to all week, and the whole house would be smelling like popcorn by now.

Margaret could have arranged to carpool with someone. She had decided to drive to the museum by herself so she could stay at the party as long as Edward did. A comfortable drizzle was coming down and it was still light out when she parked the car and walked up the steps to the museum.

The campus art museum was a fine brick, baroque-style building. It had a good reputation for hosting traveling exhibits and had recently shown an important exhibit of communist propaganda art. Edward had been director of the museum for four years now, and Margaret felt he was perfect for the job. It had been easy for her to manage a place on the board since her doctorate was in Pacific Northwest native art. She worked at the nearby Princess Angeline Museum, and had had extensive board experience over the years in many volunteer jobs. Edward had no say in her appointment, so she never felt there was anything improper in her placement. He was delighted to have Margaret on his board and assumed she would agree with him on all the important issues.

Of course he was right about that. She had agreed with him for several years, that is until recently when she had refused to go along with his plan to exhibit some Russian Constructivist art. It had all happened by accident really; she simply disagreed with the proposal before knowing who had proposed it.

But then after thinking it over a bit, she realized that she really did object to the show. It seemed redundant after the Constructivist show, so she decided to stick to her guns.

At first Edward was shocked and surprised by her opposition. Then he began to ignore her in a very obvious way that reminded Margaret of a lovers' quarrel they had once had years ago. This wasn't all that bad for her since being thought of as a lover was better than being treated like a dependable old friend, or like a dog. She found that it was actually a nice change from the routine of the past few years.

Since Margaret hadn't responded to his pouty behavior Edward quickly switched gears and began to pay more attention to her. Two weeks ago, after a board meeting, he had actually asked her out for coffee. Margaret was surprised at first and even ordered a mocha by mistake, but later at the table she took no time at all figuring out why he was suddenly gazing into her eyes and asking about the last tune-up on the Mercedes. She quickly calculated that she could possibly afford to disagree with Edward on some museum policy about once a year and reap the benefits for several weeks afterwards.

In the museum gallery Margaret saw the usual faces. Spouses as a rule managed to avoid this event so she glanced around hoping that Edward's wife, Annette, wouldn't be there. Her heart sank a little, however, as she heard Annette's confident voice from across the room. Turning around she saw her laughing heartily with the chairman of the museum board and the director of the university. She was dressed as always when not wearing her athletic wear, with perfect taste in her own style that defied categorizing. Only her hair seemed a little odd. It was all messed up in one of those new hairstyles movie stars always seemed to wear when they got married.

"How you doing, Margaret?" A familiar voice in a soft, low southern drawl interrupted her thoughts.

"Hello, Matt, I'm fine," she turned and answered with a warm smile. Her best friend Nel's husband was a local artist who was known for glass sculpture. Although Matt had grown up in the nearby blue-collar city of Everett, he had a sweet country-like demeanor and a distinctive drawl.

"Is Nel here?" Margaret glanced around the room to look for Nel.

"No. She wants you to call her though; she's working on a new project."

"Oh, really?" Nel, who had earned a doctorate in socio-cultural anthropology, but was also an artist and had done several shows of her own that emphasized strong feminist themes.

"Yeah, she's gonna start selling Avon."

"What?" The volume of Margaret's voice startled several people around her. "How can she do that?"

"She says it has to do with some African tribe or something, the Woodabe tribe, I think."

Margaret was relieved. Perhaps it had to do with the urbanization of rural Africa. "Is she going to Africa then?" Going to Africa was a common occurrence among socio-cultural anthropologists, and nothing that Nel did could be surprising, except perhaps selling Avon.

"You just call her." He raised his hand as if to distance himself. "I'm staying out of this one." Nel was well known for unusual projects that required the intense involvement and passion of her friends, but it was impossible to think of her selling Avon products, even in urbanized Africa. Of course, money had been a big problem with them this year. The image of Nel dressed in an ethnic tunic and wearing earrings from Cameroon, ringing a doorbell and calling out "Avon" crept into Margaret's mind. It was impossible. There must be some other explanation.

"I'll call her tomorrow." She scanned the room one more time; she still hadn't seen Edward. As she surveyed the gallery, Margaret was surprised to see Pablo Koplan, one of the city's premier art critics, walking towards them. He was a stocky man in his early fifties with a moustache and dark, slightly greasy hair that he combed straight back. Although he was balding, he had managed to keep up a youthful appearance with a small ponytail. Margaret had known him for years, ever since she and her sister Joan were graduate students at the university. He had been a professor of art history then and had taken a special interest in Joan.

"I thought we got shed of him. Didn't he move to the Big Apple?" Matt's tone was almost hateful.

"His home base is still here." She was barely able to answer before Pablo was upon them.

Margaret, immediately realizing the importance of such a man to Matt and his work, introduced them and quickly began detailing the highlights of Matt's career. Pablo listened, nodding his head and pulling at his moustache as he glanced around the room, but his interest waned quickly and Margaret could hear herself talking faster and louder as she tried to include all Matt's artistic triumphs. And Matt, who could have offered a few facts, wasn't helping any by sucking the meat out of a crab claw that he had grabbed off a nearby buffet table.

"Matt will be the featured artist at the art auction that Joan is planning in August." She was almost breathless by the time she finished.

"Joan?" Pablo looked at them for the first time since he had joined their conversation. "Ah, yes, Joan," he mumbled almost to himself. Margaret wondered if he only just now realized who she was. It had been a year since she had seen him at Joan's last open house, but at least she had suddenly gotten his full attention.

"Almost the entire exhibit will feature local glass work. Glass has certainly put us on the art map, hasn't it?" she went on. "Anyway, I'm sure Joan would love to give you a private tour before the show opens next month. Anything you could do would be so helpful, and of course all the money goes to the children."

"Yes, of course. I would be happy to help Joan. Have her call me as soon as possible." He reached into his pocket and gave Margaret his card.

Margaret beamed as he handed it to her. She felt she had made quite a coup. Not only had she promoted Matt, now Pablo was interested in the art show. Pablo's enthusiasm was obvious, she mused, glass art is everything in this town. How fortunate for Matt to be in on the ground floor.

"Thank you so much," she gushed, grinning from ear to ear. "It's such a good cause and"

"By the way, I saw your nephew last Friday," Pablo interrupted her.

"Her nephew? You mean Fred?" Matt finally decided to join their conversation. Of course Nel would have told him all about Fred's problems, which was fine with Margaret since they all had seen Fred grow up, but why couldn't Matt show a little interest in his own career? He was just like every other artist she knew, always leaving the burden of promoting their work to friends and family.

"Yes, yes, Fred. Joan has a son named Fred. I've met him several times." Pablo gave Matt a scornful look. "I saw him on the ferry, I was with some people from New York."

"Ferry?" Margaret tried to think why Fred would be on a ferry.

"He was with a woman. I thought it was a man at first, but they were kissing."

"Was she very thin, with short sandy hair?"

"Yes, looked like a boy, but she was definitely a woman. He was holding her buttocks, and she was pushing her body against his. They were kissing in a very sensual way and..." His details were beginning to make Margaret feel a little uncomfortable. Perhaps, as Fred's aunt, she should make some excuse for such a public display.

"It must have been his wife, Susan. That's just what she looks like," she said, defensively, as she glanced over to Matt. His scornful glare at Pablo startled her a bit. "I'm surprised they would act like that in public. It's really not like them at all." But that explains why he hasn't been over lately, she thought; how nice that they were back together. They certainly must have been carried away by their reconciliation though.

"But it wasn't really in public; they were in a kind of alcove on the upper deck, and the weather was bad so no one was up there. Anyway, then your nephew sat down and the woman straddled him on his lap. Her hand..." he tried to continue but he suddenly began to make a low guttural noise that seemed to be coming from somewhere in the back of his throat.

"Are you all right? Are you choking?" Margaret reached for his hand as Matt began to pound on his back.

"Yes, yes, I'm fine," Pablo blurted out. He waved them both away with an irritated gesture and then hurried off, pushing his way though the crowd. He was still wheezing as he made his way across the room.

"Do you think he's all right? Look, he's gone into the bathroom. Matt maybe you should check on him."

"He's fine. He's such a sleazeball."

Margaret's eyebrows arched in surprise. Here was a man who could make or break his career. Of course, Pablo was a little sleazy with his greasy hair and all but Matt should do more to promote himself. It was easy to see why Nel was always complaining about his laid-back attitude, and saying he would never get ahead of the game. It would be no wonder if Nel was forced to sell Avon.

The party continued on in a lively manner, but once Margaret located Edward, she preferred to be more of an observer than in the fray. As she stood back looking at the crowd, she began to wonder how an artist might paint the scene. But there was no hazy smoke floating through the room that could be washed across the canvas, giving the romantic air that was needed. In fact the light was rather bright and harsh, and the people seemed unattractive and sharp. Perhaps Albright could do it justice, she decided, as she cocked her head sideways a bit and squinted.

Moving around the perimeter of the room, she found several opportunities to eavesdrop on some interesting conversations and was sure that one of the bigwigs from the University board was getting drunk. She kept a eye on him for some time and even noticed that he wasn't wearing his wedding ring.

It wasn't until the end of the party after most of the people had left that she felt comfortable going up to Edward to say hello. Of course they were interrupted almost immediately so Margaret moved on without Edward noticing.

Although the event was catered, the budget was unfortunately small, so the caterers had put the

*"Anyway, then your nephew sat down and the woman
straddled him on his lap. Her hand…" he tried to
continue but he began to make a low guttural noise
that seemed to be coming from somewhere in
the back of his throat.*

food on disposable plates and left early. Anyone from the board who was still there at the end would be expected to help clean up so Margaret started to cover the leftover appetizers with some acid-free tissue she had found in the storeroom of the museum. As the museum emptied out, she began to feel a little nostalgic; here they were, the three of them, Annette, Edward, and herself, working side by side as they had done so often before. They had spent all those years sharing school, work, and friendship; they were almost like a family, if one really thought about it.

"Oh, you don't need to do that." Annette's sharp tone startled Margaret. "No one will eat those leftovers unless you and Helen want them."

"Well, I just didn't want to waste"

Annette shoved a large, black plastic garbage bag towards her. "A much more efficient use of your time would be to dump everything in here."

Margaret began dumping. "Did you get a chance to talk to Allen Angston from the Met? That new show of theirs is fabulous." Edward was suddenly at her side. He leaned back and waved his hands as he began to discuss the merits of outsider art and how it should be accepted by the museum world.

Margaret stopped cleaning to listen; she noticed the familiar sparkle in his eyes that came over him when he discussed art. It was such a pleasure to hear him talk, she thought, as she gazed up at him. "…and they actually let Hub Cap Joe curate the entire thing. It's fabulous," he went on. Margaret tried to agree with him when she could get a word in, but it wasn't easy.

*He was still so attractive with his
beautiful dark hair and deep blue eyes
that it took her breath away.*

"Edward, please," Annette interrupted them as she wheeled a large trash dumpster across the room. "I really don't want to be here all night."

Margaret started to clean up again as Edward moved away whispering, "I'd help you but I don't want to splatter any food on this new linen suit."

While Margaret and Annette finished cleaning, Edward disappeared into his office until it was time to lock up the museum. When they were done, the three of them walked out to the parking lot. It was still drizzling lightly as they made their way across campus and this added to Margaret's already pensive feelings. "What a beautiful night," she heard herself say.

"You'll probably have to have that suit pressed every time you wear it." Annette's tone was rather bitter and Margaret felt a little embarrassed at being a witness to their marital strife. Edward glanced down at the wheat colored linen suit with a concerned look on his face.

"This rain certainly isn't helping it. I should probably get a summer raincoat to wear over it, something in a darker tone of this shade. What do you think, Margaret?"

"That would be nice." She stopped to look at his suit and their eyes met. He was smiling at her and his face was glimmering along with the street lights that were reflecting in the water on the ground. He was still so attractive with his beautiful dark hair and deep blue eyes that it took her breath away.

"Well, good night." Margaret watched as he and Annette split apart and got into their separate cars.

"'Night," he called out back. It was indeed a beautiful evening, she thought, as she drove home through the misting rain.

CHAPTER VI

*F*n the car alone, Edward readjusted his rear view mirror so he could see the cars behind him. As he turned onto the street, he caught sight of Margaret's car pulling out of the parking lot. Maybe he should call her tomorrow and take her out for coffee again. He still couldn't believe she had voted against his proposal at the May board meeting. The other members were shocked as well, and he didn't want a repeat of that awkward moment following the vote, when no one knew what to say or do. He wasn't even sure if she still loved him any more, or if he appealed to her at all. They were, after all, over forty and Margaret had remained single and attractive all these years while he had gotten married and even had children. It could be that she had hooked up with some young artist type at the museum.

Things like that happened. Or maybe he wasn't as attractive as he use to be; his wardrobe or his looks might have slipped a little lately. At a stoplight he moved the mirror so he could see himself again.

After a few more seconds of contemplating his reflection in the evening light he felt reassured. Margaret had after all, seemed like her old self again tonight. Of course they would always be good friends, but friendship obviously wasn't enough to insure her board vote. As these thoughts nagged at him, he started to feel resentful.

He had enjoyed Margaret's devotion for so long and had been telling himself that on his part at least their relationship was simply a brief college romance that had developed into a close friendship. Of course, he knew she had loved him, loved him in a way that he had never felt for her or really for anyone, but he had decided long ago that that part of their relationship was of no consequence, and that it could easily be separated from the friendship part. This rationalization allowed him to ignore her feelings in a way that conveniently suited his needs.

After all, it was fun to be idealized by someone, especially if you weren't obligated to give back much in return. Until the May board meeting, their relationship had gone on in this easy way for so many years. Of course, if his own wife was not so busy with all her tennis and aerobic activities, he might not need to rely on Margaret's attention so much. He thought dejectedly about how all his friends and colleagues viewed Annette as the perfect mate: so attractive, fit, and athletic. Everyone agreed, in a superficial way, that he was lucky to have such an exquisite companion.

Annette had grown up in Lakeview and had inherited quite a bit of money of her own, which was convenient for Edward, whose salary was small, but it did lead to a certain independence that Edward found irritating. He felt at times that she wasn't taking care of him as she should.

Lately, he had been wondering why she had married him in the first place and why he'd married her. She certainly didn't share his interest in modern art, at least not any more. It was disgusting the way she let her whole life be consumed with maintaining her appearance. Oh sure, he liked to look nice too, but it wasn't the only thing he ever thought about. Anyway, clothes had such an artistic element and not all the narcissism that came with being obsessed with your muscle tone.

When he thought about it though, Annette's looks, and the self confidence and power that came from her appearance, were probably the only things she had going for her. It was disconcerting for him to think that was the only reason everyone respected her. If people ever found out how superficial she'd become, it could be embarrassing. One should at least have the pretense of a higher calling.

And then there was Annette's attitude toward his new BMW. Edward glanced around his car with pride. He wished she would stop slamming the doors so hard and leave enough space in the garage to park it safely. You'd think she would understand better when he needed to park it over on the empty side of a parking lot so no one would bang car doors against it. With all the exercising she did, she shouldn't complain about walking across a parking lot. She had once even called it a phallic symbol. And she certainly didn't take the care she should with his wardrobe either.

The women in his life were definitely neglecting him lately. It was frightening for him to think a pattern might be developing, or maybe some kind of conspiracy. His palms became sweaty at the thought of it all, and he was shocked to notice that the leather cover on his steering wheel was becoming blotchy. He took a deep breath and pulled over so he could dry his hands with a tissue.

Back on the road, he tried to compose himself but a jogger brought his thoughts back to Annette. Her athletic abilities were astounding, but even that had caused him considerable embarrassment. Like the time, two years ago when she had climbed to the top of Mt. Rainier unknown and ahead of him.

When he had arrived at the top of the 14,410 foot peak, barely alive and able to stand up, he had found her women's climbing group waiting with a picnic basket, complete with wine laid out on the glacier. The local papers loved it and ran a front page story in the *Scene* section with a photo of Annette sitting in a folding chair handing him a glass of wine. It was a beautiful photo of her looking relaxed and content while he was visibly haggard.

The publicity had been good for the museum, but he felt it had diminished his own achievement and humiliated him as well. Margaret would never have embarrassed him in that way, he decided as he squeezed into the garage next to Annette's car. He was glad she had beaten him home. If Annette had pulled in after him, she probably would have banged her car door against his and chipped the paint. He opened the door a few inches and crawled out of his car; tomorrow he would try and talk her into parking on the street.

CHAPTER VII

ouise Marston sat on the deck in her backyard, pen and paper in hand. From her isolated perch, well hidden among the trees, she had a clear view down the short street, which started at the lake and then dead-ended at her property. First in sight was Joan and Bill Philbrick's house across the street, where all the goings-on of the family were easily discernible; next, she could survey all the cars passing up and down the street; then there was the vacant lot with the basketball court, an active spot in the summer, and from there her eyes drifted up to her little patch of blue, the lake.

Louise had long since reconciled herself to the fact that her prominent neighbor, indeed the most prominent citizen in the city, billionaire Bill Gates, had moved from the house just to the right of the basketball court. Although she knew the status of her deck would never be the same, she felt it would always be an impressive thing that if one stood at the edge of the deck and were willing to lean out far enough and turn at just the right angle, one would be able to make out the weather vane that topped what used to be Bill Gates's boat house, and of course his laurel hedge was clearly visible even when sitting comfortably in a chair.

But, even though these tidbits of him would remain, Louise knew there was a huge difference between having Bill in the flesh, and having a hedge. She would always miss seeing his seaplane land on the lake amid the myriads of water-skiers and their boats. On more than one occasion, she had imagined herself testifying in court, on Bill's behalf of course, that his plane had clearly had the right of way when it landed on the lake and maimed that irresponsible skier who was obviously at fault.

Naturally, the fantasy would continue, since Louise was always thinking of others, that Bill would be so grateful to her for saving him all those legal inconveniences and would feel obligated to attend her next fund-raiser or make a sizable donation to her favorite charity. Then they would have become best friends, and it was impossible to imagine the bliss and status she would have enjoyed. But, she thought, as she dejectedly watched the water-skiers safely zipping back and forth across the bay, it will never happen now. She shook her head in dismay and stared at his hedge. She had never been able to get a cent out of the illustrious billionaire, even for the neighborhood park improvements. Hadn't he himself grown up in the neighborhood and perhaps, if one really stretched the imagination, hadn't he maybe even once played at the park itself? But now he had moved away across the lake to horrid Bellevue. She had to check herself, as a good Christian woman, from thinking all the odious thoughts that came to her mind when she remembered that Bill had moved over to the east side of the lake. Better not to dwell on it.

Louise glanced up to the University football stadium that loomed above the lake and smiled as she thought back to how she had successfully ruined Joan's Octoberfest. How easily she had managed it. How silly of Joan not to check the Huskie schedule, and how lucky to have an unusually late game that day. Thank goodness for network TV's influence over college football, she mused. Of course, there would be no real chance of changing the date of the event. The Philbricks would be gone at the end of the month and nobody ever heard of an Octoberfest in November. No, it would have to be back to square one, a croquet party at the park in August with everyone dressing up in Victorian costumes and sipping tea, instead of lederhosen and gorging on knackwurst, how disgusting that would be. Her body shivered at the thought of it.

Not feeling inspired by her pen and paper, she turned to look back with admiration at her house. It was indeed a small house, less than two thousand square feet, but it had been redone, or 'restored' as she liked to say, to perfection. She had tried to resign herself to the fact that although the interior of the house was in the charming French Normandy style, the outside had a much more common Cape Cod appearance. When she first began her restoration, she had envisioned fortifying the exterior with stones and adding a Norman tower, since she felt that the more elite interior French style should be allowed to flow onto the exterior structure. Her initial plan had been abandoned, however, much to her husband's relief, because of its expense.

Instead, a single picket fence had been installed in the front and around the deck closest to the house in the back. This deck was now to be called the 'back porch', a term much more fitting for a Cape Cod style house than the term 'deck', which indicated a more modern, even Californian style of architecture, that wouldn't do at all. The different styles, French Normandy and Cape Cod, would be one more of the many interesting things to comment on about the house, she rationalized.

As with many of her friends and neighbors, Louise had given up several years of her life to restoring and perfecting her house. Once finished, most people would just sit back and enjoy the fruits of their labor, but Louise couldn't conceive of such an idle luxury as a free minute since she was such a tireless worker for the community. And for that matter, a house was never really done, as she had so often reminded her friends. She picked up her pencil and wrote on her pad: 1. Paint tile in upstairs bathroom (something she had been planning to do for years). That pale yellow would have to go. Then she looked back out towards the water, waiting for more inspiration. She was excited to see a couple of sea planes circling over the water skiers. Maybe she could be of service to some other billionaire; there were so many of them around these days.

Although Louise was only one half block from the lake, her view was a small one thanks to a giant deodara cedar in the northeast section of Joan's yard. Since she had moved into her house five years ago, Louise had spent much of her time in a state of agitation over this particular tree. It blocked not only most of her lake view from the outside deck but also her entire lake view from all the upstairs bedroom windows where the view would have been panoramic. When she first moved in, her plan had been to offer to pay the Philbricks to have the tree cut down and removed.

This seemed like a simple solution, but of course she had known Joan for several years and knew it would be humiliating for her if Joan rejected the idea, as Louise thought she might. The key to success would have to be the insipid Dr. William Philbrick. With him in mind, Louise had spent two hours one Saturday morning four years ago looking out her upstairs window, waiting to see when Joan would leave the house. She had then rushed across the street, fresh blueberry muffins in hand, and wasted another hour with the 'idiot,' as she was to call Bill Philbrick from that day on.

Louise had listened to him intently, bored to death but with a simpering smile on her face, as the Doctor described in detail how he was in favor of having the tree removed since he spent most of his Saturday mornings sweeping the needles off the sidewalk and street. He also complained that it had ruined his front lawn because the water evaporated in the upper branches before it reached the ground and when he watered the grass, it just sucked all the moisture from the turf. It also blocked out every ray of sunshine and grass needed sunshine. Then there were the roots which caused the lawn to be uneven by clawing their way above ground.

Also, he wasn't able to park his car in front of
the house because of all the debris that fell from
the tree. The needles had also caused difficulties
with the house to the north of the Philbrick's, since
those neighbors always swept them into a nice
heap and then returned them each week to the
same exact spot on the Philbrick lawn. One of the
neighborhood dogs had become particularly fond
of the pile. Bill made Louise walk around the side
of the house so she could observe the mound of
needles that, sure enough, did have a deposit from
the neighbor's Black Labrador adroitly placed on
its top. Louise and Bill stood looking at it for a few
seconds. Oddly, she felt at a loss for words. Her
mind drifted back to a trip she had taken to Greece
last summer, all those acropoleis scattered around
the countryside with columns either tumbled over
or standing up straight. These would probably be
Doric, she decided as she looked down on the pile.

"But the worst problem of all is with the gutters
and the roof of the house," Bill complained, turning
their attention away from the pile and back up to
the house and the tree. He pointed to the gutters
and lamented that he was forced to clean them
out several times a year because of the needles.
They also wreaked havoc on the roof. He was sure
they would have to replace it soon.

Louise had been all sympathy and kindness as
she listened to the Doctor. She couldn't agree
more. The tree must go. He was so distraught by it
that she started to regret she had ever offered to
pay for its removal at all. She began to calculate the
most graceful way to retract her offer; perhaps she
could just pretend to forget she had ever proposed

to pay in the first place. After all, once the tree was gone the Philbricks would be too proud to ask her for the money anyway. But before she was able to form her plan, the Doctor told her what she should have known in the first place: that it didn't matter in the least what he thought. Joan wouldn't hear of the tree's removal, and there was absolutely no chance the tree would ever come down. He had given up asking her to have it removed. Louise gave out a loud sigh. She had known enough of the Philbricks even then to realize that if Joan wanted the tree, then no matter what the Doctor thought, Joan would keep the tree.

This had been a heavy blow to Louise. She retreated to her own home and blamed her husband Brian for Doctor Philbrick's inability to stand up to his wife.

"It's a male bonding thing. You should go over there and coach him on how to be a man. Why can't that silly idiot have any say in his own house?"

Brian had looked at Louise. He wanted to laugh out loud at the idea of himself coaching any husband on standing up to his wife. He had given up on that years ago. Without answering her he had walked over to the living room window and looked out at the tree. Its massive trunk was split in two almost at ground level and then formed into two handsome columns. Brian felt curiously sorry for the poor thing. There it was, rooted to its spot, surrounded by these two petty women. He watched as a breeze caught the branches. It seemed to wave to him in a kind of weak commiseration. He remembered an old Native American chant he had learned at camp when he was a child, *Oh, cedar tree, clap your hands and dance with me.* But this wasn't a proud native species: it was a transplant. An extraneous cedar trying to cope in a hostile environment.

He thought of the doctor and his relationship with his wife. How easy it was to understand why Bill hadn't prevailed with Joan. He imagined himself talking things over with Bill, maybe even sitting in a friendly bar someplace and drinking a glass of beer, but he knew things wouldn't go as Louise envisioned. There would be no change as far as the tree was concerned. He shook his head and reached for the string that pulled the curtains closed. It would be better to ignore Louise and try to stay out the whole mess, he decided.

After Louise had finished venting her anger on her husband, she plunged into Plan B for the tree removal: the tree's state of health. But the more she read about the tree, the more disgusted she became. Not only did the species live to be a thousand years old, but it wasn't even native to this country. Since the neighborhood, eminent as it was, had been settled only at the turn of the century, the tree could well live until the year 3000. She had also read that unlike the Pacific dogwood, no common blight could be introduced to infect the tree. Indeed the deodara was amazingly resilient. Heavy snow did at times weigh down and break off branches, but a good snowstorm only happened about once every five years or so, and wind storms usually had no effect whatsoever.

Louise had then sunk into a state of depression. It was too much to think of the beautiful lake view that the Philbricks enjoyed from their house when all she could see was the horrible, ugly branches of their massive deodara. As her desperation increased, she began to explore the legal consequences of tree vandalism. She could pretend she lived in their house when they were on vacation and have it cut down. What about copper nails? She had heard about them killing trees. If she did it at night, no one could ever prove it was her. Even if she did get caught, so what, the fine couldn't be that much. Besides, it would easily add twenty-five thousand dollars to the value of her house to have the view.

Although her husband, Brian, had no ideas of his own to offer, he did not support any of Louise's. After becoming alarmed at some of her suggestions, he consulted an attorney, or so he claimed.

"The court could charge you up to fifty thousand dollars, and you could be put in jail," he warned her. "Or the Philbricks might sue us for any amount of money they want."

For the first time in their marriage, he had actually put his foot down and even used the word "forbid" to her. When Louise asked him how long her sentence might be, he only answered, "Would you really want the whole neighborhood to know you were serving time in jail, no matter how short the term, because you had cut down Joan's tree?" She knew he had her on this point, because even with the tree gone, Joan would have the last word if she was in jail, and that wouldn't do at all. Louise couldn't give her the satisfaction.

Louise had spent the next two years despondent over the tree. She felt completely at a loss. Her ideas had run out, and her husband had abandoned his support for her. Every morning she awoke in her bedroom to see the branches of the mammoth deodara spread out before her. In the summer she would catch fleeting glimpses of water-skiers and sailing regattas, only to have them disappear behind its massive branches. In the winter when every other decent tree lost its leaves, there it stood blatantly, with all its foliage intact. Windstorms were not strong enough and snowstorms not heavy enough.

And Joan never missed a chance to rub the whole thing in any time she got the opportunity. 'Beautiful sunset,' she'd sweetly call out from her yard, or 'Did you see the eagle fishing this morning?' Louise was beginning to feel that Joan kept the tree out of spite and maliciousness alone. Joan was just a nasty, vicious woman. Everyone else thought she was so wonderful with all her good works for the community, everything always being so organized, but Louise knew better, and she became determined that everyone else should know, too.

Sitting on the deck, Louise sighed as she watched a seaplane disappear behind a branch. She began to fantasize that with a rifle, a laser gun, or a pair of sharp pruners and a very large ladder, she would be able to clip that branch and increase her view by forty to fifty percent. That was all it would take to improve things for her, but she knew she would never get the opportunity. Instead, all that was left for her to do was to wait pathetically each year for August to come around, when the tree was always pruned by Tex's Tree Service.

Sitting on the deck one day last summer when the pruners were working, she had anxiously watched to see if this time they might just happen to cut the right branches to increase her view; but as they had finished their work and began packing up, she had known this would not be her lucky year. With the slight hope of seeing some improvement from the house, she had gone inside to have a look.

It was there, at the upstairs window, that she had gotten, as she later described to Colleen, 'a spontaneous overflow of powerful feeling' that swept over her body. A plan was hatched. This inspiration had loomed in importance to her not only because it was brilliant, which of course it was, but because of the two year gap there had been since her last good idea regarding the tree. It was frightening to think how long it had taken her to get the creative juices flowing again, and how pathetically close she had gotten to surrendering to Joan.

Of course, it was to take yet another year before she could put her plan into action, but now that year had passed and it was time for her to make her move. Joan would not have the last word, Louise determined as she put down her pen and paper and looked down at her watch. It was 11:30 and the Philbrick's car was still gone but they would be returning home from church any minute. She decided to wait out on the deck for a little longer so she could watch them return and perhaps even overhear a bit of their conversation. Also, her husband Brian was busy cleaning up debris from a recent windstorm and it was pleasant to sit and observe him work.

As she watched, she began to reflect on her latest scheme regarding the tree. Having a new plan, and knowing that it was waiting to be put into action, had given her the courage to go forth and attack Joan's power within the guild. During the past year, Louise had had to sit by and watch her take over the guild. True, it was Joan's turn to be president that year, and everyone had to do it once, but Joan had exploited her authority over the other women to the point where Louise was outraged for both herself and the others.

Louise had started out the year opposing Joan as she went along, but the other guild members seemed to dislike any kind of confrontation so much that Louise gave up defending them. 'What a bunch of weak sisters!' she had told her husband. She knew, however, that her turn to be president would come next year and that if the other members' lack of courage to oppose the president continued, she would easily have her own way. Louise's time would come, and Joan would just have to get used to being under her control for a change.

Hearing a car door slam, she stood up and crept off the deck to a hiding point behind the fence. She watched as the Philbricks got out of their car and walked into the house. They must have gotten home from the auction early last night if they had gone to church, unless Joan went just to brag to everyone about how tired she was after going to the Blanco Auction, or more likely to crow about what they had bought. By now she has probably figured out why we had to change the date of the Octoberfest, but there is nothing even Joan can do about a college football game.

She moved back over to the deck and picked up her pencil: "2. Croquet party," she wrote on her list, feeling as if she had finally gotten the best of Joan for the first time in years.

CHAPTER VIII

There was no rain that Sunday morning until about eleven o'clock when it started to drizzle. By lunch time the drizzle had turned to intermittent showers. After her lunch, Margaret realized without really caring much that she had spent most of the morning trying to stay busy in the yard so she could avoid calling Nel. The idea of calling her to ask if she was going to start selling Avon nagged at Margaret on and off all morning. She couldn't decide what to say.

Since it was sunny during the morning, she felt obligated to work outside which was something she hadn't been in the mood for after yesterday's fuss with the rhododendron. That was the nice thing about rain, you didn't feel obligated to run outside and into the sunshine to do something you didn't want to do anyway. But at least she had managed to kill three hours doing yard work without calling Nel. The second excuse she came up with was to call Joan. She wanted to find out about the auction and to tell her about Pablo and Fred. Joan wasn't in any mood for small talk though. She brushed the auction aside quickly as being too boring and moved onto more important things.

"I found out about the Octoberfest. There's a Husky game. Do you believe it?"

"A Husky game? But how could you have missed that?" Margaret cried out bluntly as if Joan had failed to see an entire football team running past. That kind of oversight wasn't like Joan at all.

"I don't know. I guess I just wasn't thinking about football, and if it wasn't an evening game it wouldn't have mattered anyway. I mean, it is July, and I was so preoccupied with getting the thing through before Louise got back. I should never have let her intimidate me. I could have easily convinced everyone to have an Octoberfest instead of a croquet party even with her around. No one can stand her."

"Well, you'll figure it out; look at your calendar again," Margaret encouraged her. "And, anyway, guess what I heard? I have some news that will make you very happy. Fred is back with Susan; at least I think they're back together. They were seen kissing on a ferry boat."

"Seen kissing on a ferry boat? My God, who told you that? It sounds like it was on the news." Joan didn't seem excited about this revelation at all; in fact, she sounded incredulous. Her attitude unsettled Margaret, who thought it was the best news that any of them could imagine.

If they'd gotten back together, though, Joan would have found out about their reconciliation before Margaret would have. Joan always knew everything first.

"I heard it from Pablo Koplan. He was sure it was Fred. He said he was fondl ... I mean kissing, a girl who looked like Susan on the ferry. He also said he would review your art auction in the newspaper; you just have to call him. He gave me his card," Margaret went on, the wind dying in her sails.

"Well, it wasn't Susan."

"How can you be so sure?"

"Because, Margaret," Joan said impatiently as if she were being forced to talk about something she didn't want to discuss, "Susan is in New York, she moved there to be with her new lover. Fred came by here last week and told us that Susan has realized that she is gay and that she has moved to New York. He said he is in love with another girl, and she was probably the one he was with on the ferry. But this ferry business is very upsetting," Joan plunged on without giving Margaret a chance to assimilate anything, "because I don't want him taking up with another girl like Susan. I liked her and everything, but I don't think he should go around falling in love with people who are gay, unless they're men and he's gay, which I don't think is the case..." her voice trailed off.

Margaret didn't follow Joan's train of thought. She was still trying to imagine Susan being gay. Wasn't that something you figured out when you were a teenager? Did this explain the short hair, and the lack of jewelry and makeup? She started to add up some of the signs she had obviously missed.

"I would've told you earlier, but I just couldn't deal with telling Helen. Will you tell her for me?

She'll drive us all crazy for a week with a thousand questions. I know it."

Margaret talked to Joan for a few more minutes and then hung up the phone. She knew little more than that Susan was gay and had moved to New York to live with another woman. It was just like Joan not to feel the need to discuss the situation in detail. Joan quickly immersed herself in the present and the future; the past was finished, and it was a waste of time to discuss it.

'I do have a thousand questions,' Margaret thought as she looked at the digital clock on the microwave. It would be another hour or two before Helen got back from her weekly Sunday lunch at Burgermaster with her friends from church. Margaret stood in the middle of the kitchen trying to think how she would break it to Helen as she watched the numbers change on the clock. Perhaps Susan wasn't really gay after all but only thought she was. But then she checked herself. Who else but Susan would really know if she was gay? If Susan thought she was gay, then most likely she was.

Probably none of the family would ever see her again. How odd to have a family member one day and then not the next. They had all liked Susan, but with her living in New York there would be little chance to remain friends. Perhaps she should write her a letter, a kind and supportive note about her new lifestyle, and ask her to call if she ever came back to town. Slowly the thought that Susan never did love Fred and that she may have married him out of her own confusion came into the back of Margaret's mind. How could she put him through so much pain? Shouldn't she have known better than to marry him? But, on the other hand, Fred couldn't really have suffered that much if he was already in love with someone else. Susan had been kind to him, so you couldn't fault her there. She had even been nice to Helen, which was something no one had expected of her.

Margaret looked at the phone and wondered if it would be safe to call Nel now. If she waited too long she knew she would pay dearly for it. Nel would either give her the cold shoulder and not bring up the Avon business herself, thereby forcing Margaret to say in a phony, casual manner 'I heard you'll be selling Avon,' or she would lash out immediately and say, 'Thanks a lot for calling. Were you afraid I was going to ask you to buy some lipstick or something?'

Then there was the African aspect to consider: perhaps Nel was packing her bags at this moment to do important research. But that seemed so farfetched, unless of course there was a grant for research from Avon. Maybe Matt had gotten everything all wrong. He didn't know anything about Avon. With these last two doubts minimizing her worst fears, she moved towards the phone. If Nel was in the right mood, she might even be able to get in a good talk with her about Fred and Susan. With that thought in mind, though, Margaret paused and moved back to the table to sit down.

What line should she take in telling Nel about Fred? She knew that Nel would probably take a global, artistic attitude and say something like 'So what, that's great. Hey, maybe we should all become gay and move to New York; that would solve half the problems in the world,' when

Margaret just wanted to talk about the personal aspects of the whole thing, like how long Fred had known, and how to break the news to Helen. There were so many things to consider, and there was no use expecting to have a decent conversation with Nel about it. She would just make a few jokes and change the subject. No, it would be better not to tell her at all, she decided. Nel was a good friend and fun to be around, but she seemed to have a hard time relating to other people's problems. To her, trivial things were always more important than the important things. Everything always got switched around with Nel.

At last she took a deep breath and dialed Nel's number. It was ridiculous to feel this way, but Margaret listened to each ring with a growing sense of relief. By the fourth ring, she was completely relaxed. As she left her name on the answering machine, she felt a little guilty about being so relieved at not having to talk to her best friend. So often Nel was in the kind of mood where she would disagree with anything anyone said to her or would get one idea stuck into her head so that there was no getting through to her. But Margaret didn't have long to feel guilty or relieved because her phone started to ring as soon as she hung up. She knew immediately that it was Nel calling back. It was just like her to screen her calls. Margaret quickly dismissed the idea of not answering the phone, since after all she had just called her. Now she was stuck. Margaret picked up the phone.

"Matt said you were going to Africa to sell Avon." She plunged in as soon as they had both said hello.

"I'm selling Avon but not in Africa. The first place I'm gonna hit is Lakeview, so get me a list of all your wrinkled friends over there with fat checkbooks. Hey, aren't you excited about Fred being back with Susan?" Nel went on, changing the subject. "God, I can't believe that sleazy Pablo Koplan. Matt said he was foaming at the mouth about Joan. He's always had the hots for her, and he's supposed to be such an authority on art. What a joke."

Margaret had forgotten about Matt being at the museum last night and hearing everything Pablo had said. Of course, now she'd have to tell her about Susan being gay; Nel couldn't go on thinking they were back together. "But Pablo was mistaken. It wasn't Susan. They aren't back together at all. It was Fred, but it wasn't Susan."

"Well, Fred's pretty quick. What'd he do, fall in love with the first girl he met on the street? But she must look just like Susan. He must be attracted to that type of woman, that boyish type, short hair, the waif look. That's how it works, you know. People are attracted to the same type over and over, and then they make the same mistake over and over."

"Yeah." It was a relief to have Nel going on this way. That was Joan's concern, she remembered: that he would make the same mistake again and find another gay woman to fall in love with. But only ten percent of the population was gay, and hopefully most of them knew it. How odd that he might keep finding these confused women, and how strange to think they were always attracted to him.

"Did you ever find out about what happened with Susan? Maybe he'll be able to talk about it now."

"Yeah, I found out. I found out about it five minutes ago, and I just can't believe it. I'm very upset." Maybe if she made herself sound worried, Nel would be more sensitive to her situation and then they could talk it over.

"Well, what? Tell me. They found out they're twins and that they were separated at birth."

"It's almost that bad." Margaret could tell that Nell wasn't going to take any of it seriously, she was being flippant already. She slumped down into one of the kitchen chairs feeling defeated and weary, her arms crossed across her chest and the phone wedged at her shoulder. She had often been in this situation with Nel. Almost vindictively, she resolved to make her beg for the news.

"Well, are you going to tell me or what!?" Nell demanded. "Listen, if you don't tell me, I'm not going to invite you to dinner, which is why I called in the first place."

"Dinner? When?"

"On August third. Can you come?"

"If it's a Saturday, I can come. But if it's a Friday, I can't. Why are you planning so far in advance?"

"It's a Saturday. Because Tim, Annette's perfect little brother, the anesthesiologist, is back in town and Matt wants to have him over. Don't you think it's odd that they've stayed friends all this time? They're so different. Anyway, he's finally done with school after seventeen years. Do you believe that? Seventeen years since high school, and he's just going to be passing gas." They both started to laugh. It was true: anesthesiologists did just pass gas.

"I don't think you can count the Navy years in there."

"Well, they were training him, weren't they? Hey, I can count what I want. Now tell me about Susan, or you can't come."

Margaret paused, giving a long sigh to emphasize her worried state. "Susan is gay, and she moved to New York. She left him because she found out that she's gay."

"She's gay? My god, she's gay? When did she find out that she's gay?"

Margaret was relieved with Nel's reaction to the news. She sounded ready to discuss the situation and it would be much easier to get through all this with another person to talk to. She started to relax as the two of them went over everything minutely for an hour and a half, analyzing all the details of the situation.

Nel was happy to give her advice on the right line to take with Fred: "Just be supportive. That's all you can do, anyway. It's not your fault that he married so young.

"And with Helen, just tell her. Say that you have to run some errands and on your way out the door say, 'Oh, by the way, Joan wanted me to tell you that Susan is gay and she's moved to New York.' Then she'll just call Joan and bug her. Let Joan handle it; he's her son. You have to live with Helen, that's enough. You shouldn't have to manage things between them, too."

Margaret hung up the phone feeling much better. Everything was sorted out in her head now. Nel had given her very good advice, and she did have several errands she could take care of today. As soon as Helen came home from church, she would tell her and then leave the house as fast as she could. Maybe she was acting cowardly, but with Helen it usually paid off.

CHAPTER IX

*A*nnette adjusted the straps of her new exercise outfit and looked into the mirror. The gray and black color combination was perfect, but the straps and the crotch were much too tight. "Damn it," she mumbled to herself, wondering if she could still return it. She angrily tugged at the straps one more time but instead of changing into something else, she went into the kitchen and poured herself a large glass of vodka.

"I'm going for my run now," she called out as she added some ice. "Edward, did you hear me? Edward? Edward?" Her voice started to take on an angry tone as she gulped down the vodka.

"What?"

"I said I am going out for my run now." She dumped the ice into the sink and put the glass into the dishwasher.

"I heard you the first time. Did you pick up my wheat suit at the cleaners?"

"Well, why didn't you answer me? No, I didn't."

"I wish you'd show more interest in my clothes," he called out in an irritated tone.

Outside, she closed the front door and ran down the stairs of their white Colonial house. Then she crossed the street and turned into an alley, a route she had been taking every Sunday night for the past five months. Stopping next to a gray garbage can, she jogged in place for a few seconds and glanced up and down the dead-end alley. The coast was clear so she ran past the garbage cans that were lined up neatly on each side and then ducked through a back-yard gate. As she tapped on the door of the house, she could see through the kitchen and into the living room where David was talking into the telephone. He gave her a short glance and a quick wave, and then turned his back to her. She waited a few more seconds and tapped again, harder this time.

"You're early. Shouldn't you have waited until after dark?" He said a little sharply when he finally answered the door.

"It's okay." She stopped in her tracks and glared at him. "No one is around, and it's not like we've made a habit of it." Then she walked through the living room and turned down a hall way towards the back of the house. "Anyway, I've got some exciting news that couldn't wait." She glanced around to see that David wasn't following her as he usually did. He had gone back into the living room and was looking at a baseball game on the TV.

"I've got a head cold; do you mind if we watch a little TV instead?" He patted the spot next to him on the sofa.

She turned back to the living room; it felt odd to be in that part of the house. "We'd better let down the shades though. It's getting dark, and "arsenic and old lace" might peer into the windows again," she said, remembering a story he had once told her about Helen looking into his house from her rose garden.

"Oh, I don't think Margaret looks in; only Helen does."

Annette closed the shades anyway and then walked over to sit down next to him on the couch. He put his arms around her and kissed her cheek "Germs," he mumbled into her ear. "What's your exciting news?" His eyes drifted back to the game.

She glared at him incredulously for a few seconds but didn't answer his question. Instead, she crossed her arms in front of her and began looking around the room, noticing things she hadn't seen before. They hadn't spent much time in his living room; she was struck by how orderly everything was and in such good, modern taste. You could almost say that it was 'decorated.' He was different from the kind of bachelors that were around when she was single; he was like a professional bachelor really, so settled in and not at all in need of a wife to arrange his life.

She looked back to the TV, then a sudden feeling of impatience and irritation swept over her. 'Well, one thing was certain,' she decided then and there, 'if I stay involved in this relationship, it'll be on my terms. He won't be sitting in front of this stupid TV and ignoring me for long.'

"I'm planning a trip for us. I thought we'd go to Spain," she announced decisively.

"Oh, yeah?" His voice was casual, eyes still on the screen.

She reached up to his face, put her hands on each side of his head and then turned it towards her. "Yes." She looked him in the eyes and said calmly, "but I'll tell you more about it later."

"No, no, tell me now. If I'm going to Spain, I want to hear about it."

This was more like it. He wasn't ignoring her now. He was paying attention. She settled back on the sofa, her jogging suit squeaked a little on the leather.

"Well, it's an opportunity we can't pass up. My friend Monica, you know, the aerobics instructor at the gym, is going to Spain in four months and it would be easy for me to tag along with her. My brother Tim will be living with us by then so he can keep Edward company. I've got it all figured out. You could tell everyone that you were going to your mother's and then meet me there. Isn't it too perfect?" But by the time she was done talking, he was watching TV again.

"Do you trust this Monica person that much?" he wondered out loud as he turned to face her again. He had been starting to suspect, over the last month, that Annette was getting a little carried away with their relationship. Maybe she was going too far, coming over here in broad daylight and now planning this trip. The wrong move, and they could both be caught. Then where would he be?

Lately he was beginning to think that having an affair and sneaking around was really a tacky thing to do, and very seedy. How embarrassing it would be if everyone found out he was having an affair with his neighbor's wife. Going out with married women certainly had its advantages, though, and he had been lucky over the last few years. There were no strings attached, and you could save a lot of money over dating. But this was the first affair he'd had here in the neighborhood, and he was starting to see that things could backfire.

Sure, it had been fun and easy. Annette was beautiful and had a perfect body, and she arranged everything so conveniently that he never even had to leave his house. But he still had his reputation to consider. He could easily imagine all the men he knew in the neighborhood, most of them married, ostracizing him. How could they trust him again if they ever found out about this? Why, he might even get kicked out of the Thursday night basketball game. That would be devastating. He remembered a quotation someone had read to him recently about how a person's good name was all they had in the end. It was true, he decided as raised his arm to scratch his head. Your reputation was everything.

He stood up and walked across the room where he lifted up a slat in the blinds to peek outside. He enjoyed living in Lakeview, such a small town feeling, yet all the urban conveniences were close by. He owned his house, and was part of the community. Why, he had almost as much to lose as Annette did. Maybe remaining a bachelor wasn't such a good idea. Maybe it was time to think about settling down and finding a wife. He had to live in this neighborhood, too.

"I have to live in this neighborhood, too, you know, and I still want to play basketball", he blurted out.

"David, what are you talking about? Of course you'll be living here and playing basketball. I'm only talking about a week, not the rest of our lives. I've known Monica all my life, and she's the only person who knows about us. My god, you've broken into a sweat. Do you have a fever?" She felt his forehead. "Here, drink this." She handed him a glass of water from the table. "Look, I think you're pretty sick. Don't worry about this now. I'll call you tomorrow and we'll talk. I'll try you at home because I really can't see you going to work in this condition. You must have the flu." She stood up and backed away from the couch.

"Well, what about Edward? Won't he think it's weird for you to go on vacation with this Monica?"

"No, I told you, she's my best friend. I've known her all my life, and Edward and I always take separate vacations. He usually has some stupid art exhibit he wants to see." She opened the back door. "Besides, my brother Tim will be living with us by then, and he can keep Edward company. You know, the truth of the matter is… I don't really care what you do. It's not as if we're in love or anything."

He was almost relieved to hear her. "But my feeling is, you go to Spain or else." Annette's tone of casual resignation contrasted with the sound of the door slamming. By this time it was dark. He watched from the kitchen window as she slipped down the back steps and disappeared after a quick glance up and down the alley. She seemed almost eager to get away from him.

CHAPTER X

A bird caught Joan's eye as she stood at her sink unloading the dishwasher. "Go away, go away," she screamed through the glass while she pounded on the window with a wooden spoon. The bird didn't move, however, not until he had finished making his deposit on her patio furniture. It was all the fault of that birdbath the Doctor had installed last month. She had never had any problem with the patio before he put that thing in. Now all the birds in the neighborhood perched on her deck, making messes while they waited in line to take their baths. Another one landed so she rapped at the glass again, but she didn't have time run outside and scare them off. Terry and Betty were coming to clean and she needed to finish the downstairs before they arrived.

Terry Allen and Betty Johnson had grown up in a neighborhood close to the university and had lived there all their lives. The two sisters were in their late thirties and for the past six years had operated their own business cleaning houses.

Joan thought they were worth their weight in gold so she always made it a point to clean up her house really well before they came. Terry and Betty were trustworthy, did a good job, and they were always pleasant to be around. Their ability to clean a house and their dedication were legendary. They always showed up to clean no matter what. During the big snowstorm of '93, they had taken the bus around to all their houses and had even arrived on Joan's doorstep, ready to clean, with a frozen mop.

If she was still home when they got there, she would have to remember to ask them about cleaning for her neighbor, Pam. She stopped unloading the dishwasher long enough to make a note of it on her list of things to do today. Maybe she could get them to give Pam Louise's time slot. Louise needed to be punished for ruining her Octoberfest and what better way to do it than to take Terry and Betty away from her. And it would be nice to put an end, once and for all, to that trivial business about who had actually discovered them in the first place, and whose house they had started cleaning initially.

Joan slammed a plate down onto her Corian counter top, almost breaking it as she remembered how Louise had told everyone that she had found them and that she had recommended them to most of their clients. It was very irritating, especially when the truth of the matter was that Joan's mother had actually brought them into the neighborhood.

The claim for discovering them should pass down through the generations. It was Joan, not Louise, who had recommended them to most of their clients and she was very careful about the kind of people they worked for. She had already made Pam commit to a nice Christmas bonus for them.

"What they really should do is drop Colleen," she mumbled to herself as she cleared off the counter. But Joan had already tried for that when Colleen had gone off to Palm Springs for two months last year and had expected them to hold her spot without pay.

Maybe she would have better luck getting them to dump Louise, it did seem like they disliked her more than Colleen. They complained about her following them around the house, giving unsolicited tips on how to clean. And then there was the time when Louise accused them of stealing a sponge; something they would never forget. Or what about Louise's mother? They shouldn't be working for her either, she wouldn't even let them park their old car in front of her house.

Joan, being their favorite client, felt she had some right in saying who they should clean for. She kept them supplied with lots of good houses and gave them generous raises and Christmas bonuses. She was usually home when they arrived to clean, but after a few minutes' chat about all their other clients she always left to run some errands; and she never asked them to do anything extra, like wiping off the plant leaves, the way Louise did.

It was just as well, though, that Terry and Betty cleaned for Colleen and Louise because how else would she get her bi-monthly bulletin on what they were up to? Finding out about Louise and virtually everyone else she knew was almost as pleasing to Joan as having a clean house.

For the past four years Terry and Betty had been Joan's best source of information. Their stories about Karen Olsen's husband coming out of a bathroom with a washcloth over him and asking them to iron his shirt, something they refused to do of course, or Edward and Annette's arguing about his dry cleaning, were invaluable to her. Terry and Betty knew everything, and they knew it before anyone else. Maybe she could grill them on Louise and the Octoberfest. She started to write it on her list but hesitated. It was better not to put something like that in writing.

Walking upstairs to change, she paused and looked out the window on the landing. Joan smiled, feeling thankful to Terry and Betty, as she tried to make out Louise's house through the branches of the deodara in her front yard. She was grateful to them for exposing Louise's character in the first place and giving Joan an actual reason to despise her. It was back when they had first started house cleaning and didn't know much about their clients' personal lives. Louise had been in the kitchen talking on the phone to her friend, Colleen, and Betty had over heard her calling Dr. Philbrick "a fool who probably couldn't cure a sick cow much less a person."

That very same weekend Betty's cat became ill. Betty, after hearing Louise's phone conversation over the vacuum, thought that since Dr. Philbrick was a veterinarian, she might as well take her cat over and ask the Doctor for his advice. It was on a

Sunday, Joan was at church, and the Doctor was raking needles in the yard. How idiotic it was of him to invite her into the house with that cat, even if the thing was in a box with a blanket over it. Of course, it was just like the Doctor, Joan thought as she climbed the rest of the stairs, to be flattered when anyone asked him for medical advice since that was the only topic of conversation he was ever comfortable with.

Walking into their bedroom, Joan made a face as she stood looking at his dirty underwear on the floor. She had told him that it was Betty and Terry's day to clean; he should have picked up. She snatched up the underwear and tossed it into the clothes hamper that sat at the bottom of her closet, but the hamper had been moved over about six inches from where it normally stood. She made a face and sneered as she moved the hamper back to its usual spot over an ugly stain in the carpet. She would probably have to look at that stain for the rest of her life, or at least until they recarpeted the bedroom.

It was all because of the Doctor's lack of experience with animals, he had poked the poor cat's swollen side, causing it to become spooked and run upstairs. After about thirty minutes of searching, the Doctor and Betty had discovered it in the bottom of Joan's closet having kittens on her new Faragamo's. Of course, neither of them would have the heart to disturb a cat having kittens. It had taken Joan six months to get the smell alone out of her closet, and the stain hadn't budged.

Poor Betty. On their next scheduled cleaning day, Terry and Betty had come cautiously back into the Philbrick's house. By that time, Joan had heard the entire story from her husband and she was very concerned that Betty had worked herself into a state. Betty had already cleaned out the closet as much as she could and had tried to pay Dr. Philbrick for the shoes several times. Joan was ready for them when they arrived and knew it was imperative to make them feel comfortable in her home once again.

Joan was getting the idea that cleaning houses was beginning to be more trouble than it was worth to them, and she didn't want to add to the aggravation they already received from Louise and Colleen. It wasn't very pleasant work, and they could probably earn just as much money in a nice office somewhere. The last thing she wanted was for them to be upset about a pair of shoes; Terry and Betty were worth a hundred pairs of new shoes, Faragamo's or not.

"Well, how are the kittens doing?" she had greeted them at the door as they walked up the sidewalk that Monday morning four years ago.

Betty had stopped midway up the walk with a look of dread on her face. "I'm so sorry, Joan. You have to let me pay for your shoes and the carpet."

"Do not even think about it. Besides, it's not everyday that a whole litter of kittens is born in your closet. I just can't believe I missed everything."

"At least let us work today for nothing."

"No, no. There is no way you're going to do that, and the shoes are fine. They were old. I'm just so glad your cat wasn't sick. Bill would have been so useless. How funny you thought he was a vet," Joan had commented in a curious tone. She wasn't angry or offended, but they had been working for her for several months by then, and there were a lot of medical books and journals around; it seemed likely they would know what the Doctor did.

"Louise told me. I mean Louise didn't exactly tell me, but I over-heard her, or at least I thought I overheard her, telling someone on the telephone that he was a veterinarian."

"Why would she say that?" There was nothing wrong with being a veterinarian but she couldn't imagine why Louise would have said such a thing. She had known them for at least ten years, and Louise knew full well what the Doctor did. It was then that Joan's feelings of repugnance for Louise started to turn to active hostility. She knew exactly what Louise meant by insinuating the Doctor was a veterinarian and later, after she had dragged the whole story from Betty, her abhorrence for Louise was cemented. Saying that he probably couldn't cure a sick cow was outrageous. Unfortunately for Louise all this happened right before she moved in across the street from the Philbricks and wanted their tree, the one that the Philbricks were planning to remove anyway, cut down.

After she changed her clothes and did her hair, Joan turned on the fan in the attic and made one last tour of the house. Everything was finally in order for them. Looking at her watch, she decided to make a run for it before Betty and Terry arrived. The three of them usually talked for fifteen minutes or more, so by leaving early, she would have some extra time to stop off at Denise's shop and ask her about the Octoberfest. Anyway, Terry and Betty didn't clean for Louise until after they were done at her house, so there would be little chance of hearing any news from them today. She could always call to ask them about an opening for her friend Pam.

Betty leaned into the closet and began spraying the carpet with a new cleaner she had just bought. She was hoping the bleaching agent they had advertised on TV might remove the stain from the bottom of Joan's closet. Her face flushed red when she remembered watching, with Dr. Philbrick, a litter of kittens being born in his bedroom while his wife was away at church.

The Doctor had been very kind at first, but after it became obvious there was not anything he could do to help, he had become uneasy in a way that made the whole situation one of the most embarrassing moments of Betty's life. He had gotten out towels and tried to do what he could, but the cat for some reason had taken a strong dislike to him. After a few scratches, he had given up trying to help, and he and Betty just stood around awkwardly watching as the cat took what seemed like a very long time delivering her kittens.

Using a wet brush, Betty scrubbed the stain until a foam started to appear. The foam was reassuring and it gave her a little hope that this product might work, but why would this one work when none of the other stain removers had?

She looked over to the Doctor's closet door; it was closed as usual. He always made a point to close it since the kitten fiasco. Betty took a clean paper towel and began to blot the foam.

"Damn you, Louise!" She stopped blotting when the stain reappeared, then she threw the brush across the room.

"What are you yelling about?" Terry turned off the vacuum and called out from the hall. Poking her head inside the bedroom door, she made a face at Betty and rolled her eyes. "Are you nuts? When are you going to forget about that stupid carpet? And anyway, it wasn't all Louise's fault. You thought he was a vet. You got it all wrong."

But Betty felt the whole thing was entirely Louise's fault; she had been maliciously slandering Dr. Philbrick. It was obvious that Dr. Philbrick was a good doctor and a good man. He was with an important teaching hospital, as Betty had found out on the day of the deliveries, and he couldn't have been nicer about the kittens.

Of course, Betty knew that her account of his contributions and compassion during the kitten crisis had risen as Louise's character had declined, but there could be no doubt that Louise was the most repugnant of persons. She was driven by her jealousy of Joan, of her good looks, her better house, her more important husband, etc.

After several days of stewing over her deep embarrassment, Betty had decided that the only way out of the situation was to tell Joan what Louise had said. But talking to Joan would not be easy. She had only known her for a few months back then, and although Betty liked her, sometimes, especially that first day when Joan had told them how she wanted things cleaned... well, she was very intimidating. Also, it might really hurt her feelings, or it might stir up some kind of mess that Betty did not want to get involved in.

But if she didn't tell her the truth, she would never be able clear her own name. This horrible dilemma ate away at Betty day and night for a week, and after a while, Terry wouldn't even discuss it with her anymore.

"If you don't tell her, then I will!" Terry had finally shouted. "I'll never get any peace until this whole thing is out in the open."

Then they began to discuss the pros and cons of telling her, and to analyze the relationship as they knew it between Joan and Louise. It was true, Betty pointed out, they had never heard of any problems between them. The two women knew each other, that was certain, but there was no proof they were friends. So Betty became convinced that it would be no great loss to Joan if she heard the truth about Louise. Joan was very strong and could handle anything Louise had to dish out, and Betty decided that Joan had a right to know what Louise was saying about her husband.

Giving up on her latest household cleaner, Betty did take comfort in the fact that, in the end, she had told Joan the whole story. Louise would be forever punished for what she had done; having Joan angry at you was no joke. Betty would probably have felt sorry for anyone else in Louise's position, but Louise deserved everything she got.

CHAPTER XI

Since Helen was between jobs, she had gotten into the routine of getting up on Monday mornings and having several cups of coffee while she went through the want-ads from the Sunday paper. It felt good to get up early, take a shower, and then 'do' her hair in its usual short, parted-on-the-side bob. After she did her hair, she dressed the way she always did, in a khaki skirt with a polo shirt. She liked starting off the week in this organized manner, then she could get down to the business of finding a job. She used a highlighter to mark anything in the employment ads she felt might be suitable for her, like 'personal assistant to board president' or 'front office communications manager for local radio station.'

After Helen was done with the Sunday paper, she turned to the paper that came out weekly and went through that as well. This paper had started out as an underground newspaper in the sixties, but now it was more mainstream. It still had the 'alternative' or 'unconventional' jobs Helen felt were more her style. She had worked mostly as an indefinable office worker since leaving school, sometimes even as a temporary, which she enjoyed since they didn't usually fire you. But these jobs offered her little status. On the other hand, the jobs in the *Puget Weekly* were unusual, like the gallery job she had landed once. She felt that working as a receptionist in an art gallery sounded infinitely more glamorous than working as a receptionist at a fish cannery.

There didn't seem to be much in either paper this morning; she had highlighted only five by the time she was finished. After she was done with the employment sections (she always planned to do the telephoning to the employers on Tuesday), she usually took a few minutes to read through the 'personals.' Although she herself had never considered answering any of these ads, it was interesting to read about all the people out there alone in the world. Sometimes she was reminded of how she had felt when she was between relationships, like when Harry, the grocery clerk, was transferred to another store. Since meeting David, however, she read the personals with a slight gloating feeling of superiority over all those pathetic people who had placed ads. With David in her life, Helen never thought about Margaret or herself, or any of the other single people she knew, as being in need of a mate. It seemed as if they were all content with their lives and somehow above the fray. It was only those faceless people in the paper who had a need that was unfulfilled, the

'SWF seeks passionate SWM. Must enjoy films and walks in the park.'

Today, she decided to look for an ad that Susan might have placed, like 'GWF seeks mate, contact Susan.' Only one seemed likely though: 'GWF, prefers plays to the movies, the Market to Bel-Square, seeks companionship. I hate the net...' But, of course, Susan couldn't have written that since she had already moved to New York.

Why Margaret was making such a big deal about the whole thing between Fred and Susan was beyond her, Helen thought as she switched over to the SWM section. It was perfectly natural for Susan to be gay. The whole thing was fascinating; it was so similar to David's situation. But she couldn't understand why Fred and Susan had to break up. Being gay didn't necessarily mean they'd have to end their marriage. They could still be in love. She thought back to their engagement and wedding: how romantic everything was, and they had certainly looked at each other with love in their eyes then. There was no doubt they had loved each other.

Her thoughts drifted to a fantasy she used to have about her and David getting married. She still hadn't told him about Susan being gay and leaving for New York; it was hard to decide what to do. They had never really talked about David's being gay, and it might be just the thing to bring it all out into the open.

But it could change their whole relationship and she wasn't sure if she wanted to do that. Things were just fine as they were. Even if talking about him being gay did bring them closer together, there was still the chance that it could drive them apart. He might become self-conscious around her and stop coming over for dinner or even start avoiding her. It just wasn't worth the risk, she decided. He could hear about Fred and Susan from someone else.

After she was done with the personals, Helen usually took a walk through the neighborhood before lunch, but today her mind returned to *Bartlett's Familiar Quotations*, where she was up to the D's. She was excited about some of the Dante quotes: 'The wretched souls of those who lived without praise or blame.' She reread it, trying to figure out what it could possibly mean. She kept reading it over and over; it seemed like there must be a comma missing there somewhere.

The 'wretched souls' part had such a nice ring to it. And then there was 'Consider that this day ne'er dawns again.' She liked the way that sounded too, so nice and final; death was certainly in there somewhere. She added another paper clip to that page. It now had three, which meant 'definite possibility,' but she knew that none of these would do for her mother; Margaret and Joan wouldn't stand for it. They had already dismissed 'And now my soul from out that shadow that lies floating on the floor shall be lifted - Nevermore!' Joan had said that it made them sound like they were all atheist. Still, she might try the 'wretched soul' one on them. They probably wouldn't understand it any more than she did.

By the time she was done with *Bartlett's*, it was almost eleven o'clock and time to go to the store if she wanted to get something for her lunch. A feeling of panic swept over her as she realized that if she hurried, she might make it out of the house before Margaret came back from the museum. It would be so much better not to have Margaret along. She could be so bossy at the grocery store. It should have been Margaret's day off, but she had wanted to attend a curators' meeting scheduled at the museum that morning.

Helen, almost in a frenzy at the idea that Margaret could walk in at any second, switched gears and began rushing around the house in a frantic search for her purse, the car keys, and the grocery list. She found her purse and keys fast enough but quickly gave up looking for the list because Margaret had written down most of it, and Helen never liked what she wanted to buy at the grocery store anyway. Margaret was always trying to get her to stop eating sweets. Helen flew to the door, purse and keys in hand, and opened it just in time to let Margaret in.

"Sorry, I have to rush, just going out to the store." She ran past Margaret and flew up the stairs.

"Helen, I think you need to put some shoes on. You're barefoot."

Helen turned around and slowly walked back into the house, the quickness had gone out of her step. She gave Margaret a dirty look and started up the stairs to get her loafers.

"I want to come with you. Did you get the list?"

"No," she mumbled in a defeated tone from the top landing. But by the time she was back downstairs, her attitude had changed. Now she was angry at Margaret for upsetting her plans.

She jingled her keys in Margaret's face, and walked past her to the car. "But I'm still going to drive." Margaret was left to dig her keys out of her purse in order to lock the front door.

In the car, Margaret sat gripping the dashboard. She had never liked riding in the car with Helen; she drove through the neighborhood too fast, and with school out for the summer her driving was especially dangerous. Helen also tended to brake suddenly if she saw a house for sale or noticed that someone was remodeling.

"Oh, look at that! There's Annette jogging with that friend of hers, what's her name?" she asked but didn't wait for Margaret to answer. "Now, I ask you, what can they have in common? One married with a family and the other a single aerobics instructor. Look how they're talking and talking. Now, you can't tell me that they would have anything to talk about. And how does she get her hair to stand up like that?"

"It's called a layered perm. Now, keep driving, Helen. You can't just stop and stare at people." As Helen started to speed up again, Margaret saw someone waving to them out of the corner of her eye, but she was afraid to look and see who it was since she felt that when Helen was driving, she should try to keep her eyes on the road. Finally, she turned to have a quick look. "Oh, wait," she cried out. "There's Denise and Renee. Denise wants us to stop. She's flagging us down." Helen pushed harder on the accelerator, and Margaret could see Denise and Renee starting to laugh as the car sped past them. "Helen, pull over!" Helen finally slammed on the brakes and threw the car into reverse. By the time it reached them, one wheel was up over the curb and onto the grass.

"Helen! Margaret!" Denise called out loudly and stuck her head in the window. "Hey, great driving, Helen," she smiled. "Did you hear the news, ladies? No problem with the Octoberfest, it's all set. Yours truly took care of everything. We're gonna have it on Friday night instead of Saturday. It'll be great! I already talked to the band, and it's all set. Hey, did I save Joan or what? And to tell you the truth, honey, I saved us all from Louise and that stupid croquet party. What a bore that would've been." Denise stuck her tongue out and put a finger in her mouth as if to gag herself. "Listen, I won't keep you, but, Margaret, we're having a little meeting over at Joan's to plan it all out, so we want you to be there. I think it's gonna be next week, but I'll talk to you before then. Now, Helen, don't run over us, okay?" She winked at Margaret and then jumped backwards onto the planting strip with her hands waving in front of her face. As the car jerked forward, Margaret could hear her calling out "Whoa!".

At the village shopping center, Margaret was relieved to split up from Helen. After making her promise to buy everything on the list, Margaret went off to return a slip that hadn't worked out. Helen seemed a little hyped up about things today: probably something to do with David, she decided.

As she came out of the lingerie shop, she noticed that Helen was trying to steer her cart through the parking lot while she was holding a 'grande' size coffee. With only one hand free to push, it was weaving back and forth and the car keys were dangling haphazardly through the mesh of the cart. When Margaret approached her, Helen quickly let go of the handle and grabbed at the keys. "I'm still driving."

"Fine," Margaret answered in a manner that sounded to herself a little too much like one Helen would have used. She wouldn't want to start acting like Helen. "I'll have to watch that," she made a mental note to herself. As Margaret got into the car, a sudden and horrible premonition swept over her: the thought of Helen at sixty. It was truly a frightening vision. Margaret had seen plenty of very polite and pleasant people turn rather grouchy and disagreeable in their old age. What would Helen, who was so gruff to begin with, be like in twenty or so years? It was impossible to imagine her mellowing with age.

Helen got into the car and started to back up. She was driving through the lot towards the exit when she suddenly slammed on the brakes. "Oh, did you see that? That spiffy woman in the red convertible over there just took her groceries out of her cart and then shoved it into that mini-van!" Margaret looked over to see a very attractive blond getting into a red sports car.

"I don't know why she even had a cart anyway," Helen went on. "She only has one bag. And look at her all dressed up in that suit; she looks like she could be a TV anchorwoman or something. And here she is doing something like that. She should know better! She could have put a dent in that mini-van. Why, it could even belong to someone we know."

Margaret was shocked, too, but what could they do? And now the woman was in her car and wanted to back up, but their car was in the way. The woman started backing up towards them. "Let's go, Helen. She's backing into us!"

But Helen suddenly moved the car forward, towards the convertible. The woman slammed on her brakes as the two bumpers touched.

"What are you doing? Let's go."

"No. I'm not leaving until she puts her cart back. We can't have that kind of thing going on around here. She needs to put her cart back."

Margaret noticed a look of determination on Helen's face. It was a formidable look she had seen many times before, and she knew there was no point in arguing with her. Again the horrible image of Helen as an elderly person flashed through her mind. By that time, the woman had climbed out of her car. She was raising one palm to the sky in a confused gesture and shrugging her shoulders, then she slowly walked over to their car. As Margaret sank down into her seat, Helen smiled and rolled down the window.

"Are you all right?" the woman asked Helen in a confused yet patronizing manner.

Helen smiled and replied in an equally condescending way, "You need to put your cart back."

The woman leaned into the car and looked towards Margaret, who sank a little lower in her seat. Margaret noticed that even her perfume seemed authoritative.

"What?" The woman sounded incredulous.

"You need to put your cart back."

Then she straightened up. She did look like that anchor on the evening news, the blond, anorectic one. But was that the color of lipstick she wore during her broadcast? Margaret decided to have the color on the TV checked as she watched the woman look over towards her cart, which was leaning into the mini-van. Now she understood, and Margaret could see her expression change as she realized her predicament. She was furious and she started turning red. Her lipstick color didn't seem so bright now: perhaps the studio lights made her face red during the broadcast.

"Roll up the window!" Margaret whispered desperately to Helen.

"You must be nuts!" the woman yelled. If you only knew, Margaret thought with self-pity.

"You need to put your cart back." Helen's calm demeanor contrasted with the woman's growing agitation and Margaret's fearful cowering. The woman's hand began to shake as she bent over again and leaned into the car, shaking her head in disbelief. Then she stood up and stormed over to the cart; she started to shove it in short jerks towards the cart return. When she was done, she turned back to them and started to make a common hand gesture, but Margaret looked away in time and didn't see it.

"She could have had a handgun, you know. How much coffee did you have this morning, anyway, Helen?"

"She wouldn't have a handgun, not all dressed up like an anchor-woman. Hey, maybe we'll be on the evening news; we'll have to be sure to watch it tonight." Helen threw the car into gear. "See ya on TV, honey," she called out the window.

CHAPTER XII

"W
hy bother to make coffee here, dear?" Louise purred. "You know I only drink tea. Why don't you get a latté at one of those carts next to your building or go through the drive-through at the cleaners. Then you could drink it in the car on your way to work. It'll save time and be a nice treat for you." She handed him his coat and briefcase and then moved towards the door to open it. If Brian didn't feel like a 'nice treat' this morning, he didn't say so, and Louise was easily able to shove him out the door and off to work.

"Good." She closed the door and looked at her watch. That had been a close call. The tree pruners would be there any minute, and she didn't need Brian hanging around messing things up.

Louise went to check her blueberry muffins. Poor Brian had missed having one. Too bad. But there might be some leftovers for him tomorrow morning if the pruners weren't too hungry. She began to hum as she made their coffee. When she was done, she went out to the backyard for one last look around. She had already decided on what pruning was to be done in her yard; that was the easy part. The hard part would be getting the tree pruners upstairs and into her bedroom. Louise still hadn't decided if this would be the time to do it. She could wait until they were doing their pruning at the Philbrick's and then invite them over. That might be better because if she explained everything to them today, she would run the risk of their forgetting what she wanted when they came to prune the Philbrick's tree. But then again she could always call them over to refresh their memory, in the nicest possible way, of course.

She had been asking herself these questions for the past few days and had thought, at first, that it might be best simply to establish a good rapport with them the first time around, and then apply the pressure after she had won their confidence. But then she might miss them when they came to work at the Philbrick's, and they came only once a year. If that happened, she would have wasted another whole year. No, she couldn't take that chance; better to cover as much ground as she could today and hope they weren't so stupid that they forgot what she wanted. She ran upstairs for one last look around. The bed was made, and everything was in order. She could feel her heart beginning to pound with the excitement of actually doing something, after all these years, about that awful tree.

From the bedroom window, she looked down into the yard to assess the pruning that was to be done. Brian would probably be upset about her plan to top the Japanese maple, but he'd get over it. She couldn't very well have pruners over with nothing to prune, could she? She had to come up with some work.

Then her eyes fell on a pink dogwood. It had grown taller since last year and was just beginning to block the small patch of lake that was visible from the upstairs. How natural it would sound to ask him to cut it down a bit, and what a good opening to the topic of the Philbrick's tree. She would mildly complain about how their deodara wasn't pruned enough; he would confess to doing the pruning himself, and then she would feign surprise at what a coincidence it was that he was pruning for her too.

It was then that she saw him coming through the gate and into the backyard. He was extremely tall, and in good shape for his age. He walked with a big stride that gave him a certain cowboy air. She watched as he snapped at his suspenders and looked around in a confident manner, his eyes taking in all the trees and bushes. She looked back towards the gate, but no one else was behind him. Hurrying downstairs to greet him, she went into the kitchen and finished preparing a tray with the coffee and muffins.

"You must be the tree pruner," she sang out in her most syrupy voice as she greeted him on the back porch. "Would you like some coffee and a muffin?"

"That's right, ma'am. Name's Tex." He rocked back on the heels of his cowboy boots and handed her his card. It read 'Tex, the Tree Pruner Par Excellence.'

"Turn it over," he commanded.

She read the other side, "Square Dance Caller. Do Si Do to Tex."

"I'll pass on the coffee, if you don't mind. I just had a double-short on my way over, but those muffins sure do look good. Thank ye."

"It's so good of you to come. But you're also a professional dancer: how interesting." She smiled up at him in her sweet way.

"I'm a caller and a teacher, ma'am."

"Well, maybe sometime you'll have to give me a few lessons. Are you all alone? I was thinking I'd have several of you." She sat the tray down and started to fidget with the button on her blouse. Then she smiled and looked nervously towards the upstairs window of the house.

He paused and gave her a steady look. "Well, yes ma'am, I am alone." She wasn't that bad looking except for her clothes, which looked like an old lady's. She was petite and her hair was a shiny brown. And she sure did seem friendly. "But I assure you, Mrs. Marston, I can take care of all your needs."

"Oh, please, call me Louise."

He ate his muffin and began to walk around the yard commenting on the health of her shrubbery. She followed him from bush to tree, listening intently as he pointed out all the problem areas. She made short gasps now and then, expressing her surprise at how much disease she had.

"Now, Louise, what did you have in mind to do first?" He suddenly stopped walking so that she fell into him a little, but he turned in time to catch her and prevent an awkward tumble.

"But I assure you, Mrs. Marston,
I can take care of all your needs."

"Well, this Japanese maple could do with some pruning," she said as she recovered herself, "and this Pacific dogwood is on its last leg. That horrible blight, it's too bad. But you must know all about that; I bet you just know everything about trees, don't you?" She gazed into his eyes with rapture and respect.

Tex eyed the Japanese maple. It was hard to see what she was thinking about doing with that. But the dogwood was a different story; it could probably make it through a couple more years but he was better off getting the work now if he could. Things were slow.

"But what I'm really interested in is this pink dogwood; it's blocking the view of the lake from the upstairs bedroom. I used to be able to see the lake from my bed. Maybe you could come up and have a look, and then you would know how to shape it." She gave him a big smile and formed a circle with her hands.

"Well, yes ma'am, I mean Louise, if that's what you want. I'm up for it... ah... if you are." If she meant what he thought she meant, then she sure did move fast. Lucky for him it was his first job of the day and he wasn't sweaty yet. On the other hand, she might be trying to get the bill down, and he wasn't going to go for that. But she didn't seem the type to be concerned about the bill, not living in this neighborhood.

Louise led the way up to the bedroom and walked over to the window. Gazing out towards the lake, she gave a loud sigh. "You can see the dogwood from here." But when she turned around, he was sitting on the bed. Not what she wanted at all. He needed to see which branches of the Philbrick's tree were blocking her view so he'd know where to prune it. "Come over and have a look."

"Why, your house must go street to street. You're right across from the Philbrick's..."

"Yes, we'd have such a lovely view if it wasn't for their tree. Do you know the Philbricks?" She tried to use her most naive voice.

"Well, I do all their pruning, have for upwards of ten years. But I don't really know them." They looked down through the branches. Terry and Betty could be seen carrying their cleaning supplies into the house, Joan was opening the door to greet them. Louise angrily remembered that, as always, they were due to clean her house after Joan's and she had already made her bed; what a waste of her time that was. Well, she would just have to think up something extra for them to do to make up for it. And they would still have to change the sheets!

"You do all their pruning? What a coincidence! My goodness. Can you see how just that one branch blocks our whole lake view?" She grabbed his arm and moved him closer to her so he could see it from the best position. "What a difference it would make for me to have it cut off, or just cut back a bit."

"Yeah, that's some tree, ain't it?" he laughed. "She was gonna have it removed about four year ago. I was all set to do the work but she canceled at the last minute. I don't know what happened; musta been too much money."

"She was going to do what!?" Her sweet tone disappeared again. Tex stepped back a little; this woman could get ugly. Maybe he was better off sticking to the business at hand; after all it wasn't like he was desperate or anything. There were lots of girls up at the Blue Moon who were younger and better looking than her. But then again, he hadn't been lucky in a long time. He quickly pushed from his mind the nagging thoughts he'd been having about his age lately.

"Is that the pink dogwood you were talking about?" He quickly tried to change the subject. "I don't think I would top it. Rot might set in and it won't improve your view any."

But Louise wouldn't let him change the subject. "So they were going to have it removed about four years ago. That's about the same time we moved in!" He glanced sideways at her and noticed that her body had begun to tremble. He tried to think if this shaking could mean something sensual, but it didn't seem like it.

"'Course if you really want that dogwood rounded out a bit, I could do that for you," he offered, trying to calm her down. She was starting to seem like the kind of woman you didn't want to get riled up.

Tex was relieved when she abruptly turned and went into the bathroom, he heard water running. He started to wonder what she was doing now, hoping that she was slipping into something more comfortable. Maybe she was the type that gets all riled up, and then in the mood. Just as he started to move back towards the bed, she came out. She was smiling from ear to ear but still had her clothes on. She walked back towards the window.

"Now, back to this pruning," her voice was still shaking a little. He followed her up to the window again. "I'm not really comfortable asking you for any special favors, but as you can see, I'm a little desperate here."

So that was it; he sized her up, she was counting on special favors. She wanted him to do all this work for nothing, and she was desperate to boot. Well, he wasn't that desperate unless it was for money; that's what he needed right now more than anything else. He might be able to take care of her needy parts, but he had no time for the special favors, and if he couldn't get one without the other, well then, he'd better get out while the gettin' was good.

"Well, ma'am, maybe I just better be on my way. I don't think I can be much help to you. Things is been pretty tough lately."

"What?" Louise cried out in astonishment. She hadn't done anything to justify his leaving; she had only suggested that he prune an extra branch off Joan's tree. But, of course, his allegiance would be with the Philbricks since he had been with them for ten years and everyone always took Joan's side. Franticly she tried to think of what to do. She quickly considered whether or not she should give him the money now, but then if he didn't work at the Philbrick's again for another year, she would be stuck. He might easily forget she had paid him to prune Joan's tree for her and she would never be able to prove she had given him money. As much as her view was worth to her, she couldn't abide being ripped off. She quickly decided that the best course of action would be to slow everything down a bit so that she could give him time to get to know her better. Another blueberry muffin was just what he needed.

"But you can't just leave. Let's go downstairs and you can write up the estimate for the two dogwoods and the Japanese maple, my husband may have a fit, but that's okay. We can talk about this other business another time. There's no rush, you know; it has been four years."

Four years, he thought to himself as she led the way downstairs. My god, no wonder she was desperate. Well, since he was already here, he may as well write up the estimate. You never knew what might happen. She could come into some money and besides, she wasn't bad looking.

CHAPTER XIII

argaret reread the recipe in the Julia Child cookbook for the third time just to make sure she had it right: 'blend rapidly with a rubber spatula, pressing mixture against sides of bowl.' It seemed a bit too complicated. Perhaps she should have picked up one of those pre-made strawberry pies they sell in the bread section of the supermarket. After all, it was just a potluck. She would have to remember, though, once she arrived at the party, to hide her lack of enthusiasm for potlucks. Nel would be incensed if she detected even the slightest bit of contempt on Margaret's part and she certainly didn't want to make Nel angry. Her rage could go on for months.

As she measured the flour, she began to wonder what Annette would be bringing to the party: probably just a bottle of wine or a loaf of bread. Not even Nel would have the nerve to ask Annette to cook; according to Edward, she hadn't cooked dinner in years. Of course, cooking day in and day out would be the most tedious chore for just about anyone.

It would be odd to see Annette at Nel and Matt's. They hadn't done anything together as a group in a long time unless it involved the museum, and those gatherings were so impersonal. Since she started exercising all the time, Annette seemed to be going in a different direction, as though she had grown up in some way that the others hadn't. She was so much more sophisticated and mature, as if she had figured out that there was some kind of rule or plan to life that none of the others had noticed. But with all her aerobics and weight lifting, Margaret couldn't see that Annette was any happier than the rest of them. True, her body was perfect, her house was perfect, and everyone thought she was perfect, but did anyone really like or even respect her? Margaret wondered as she worked the fat into the flour with her fingers. What was it about Annette that was so impenetrable, so impervious? Why had she held herself apart from everyone the last few years, as if she didn't have time for anyone else? Annette had become cold and distant lately, Margaret decided as she wiped the melted butter off her fingers with a towel.

Adding the ice water to the dough, Margaret's thoughts drifted back to when they used to all go to dinner together on a regular basis. Annette was one of the group back then, laughing at their jokes and comments, though she never added much herself. But lately, it seemed as though Annette thought all of the joking and wisecracking wasn't really that funny, as if her thoughts were occupied on a higher plane.

As she stirred the ice water into the flour, it went through her mind that Annette probably never really liked any of them, and that she had just been putting up with everyone all those years. Their group had always thrived on being full of nonsense and ridiculousness, in their conversation and in their humor. Margaret felt it was their most treasured asset, and Annette definitely stood out as a no-nonsense type of person.

'With the heel of one hand, not the palm, which is too warm, rapidly press pastry by two-spoonful bits down on the board and away from you in a firm, rough, quick six-inch smear.' Smear? Why couldn't she just stir? What harm could it do to stir instead of smear? She got out a wooden spoon and began to stir the dough, but after a couple of stirs she started to worry about what Julia Child would think if she could see her. Was she still alive? Could she be watching her right now? She lost her courage and began smearing with the palm of her hand, just the way Julia decreed.

Watching the messy piles of dough mount up on her marble board, she began to make excuses for Annette's selfish personality. Perhaps it was living with Edward that made Annette so disagreeable. She had always been a serious student in school, but Annette had still appreciated people like Matt and Nel, and Margaret even liked her a little back then. Now, Annette didn't appreciate anyone. Of course living with Edward with his head in a cloud about art on one hand, and his clothes and vanity on the other, could certainly have jaded anyone after all these years. 'Maybe if I had married Edward back in college, I would have ended up like Annette,' she suddenly thought as she scraped the bottom of the bowl. It was a frightening notion, yet somehow she still envied Annette. It seemed impossible not to envy someone so confident and powerful.

'Maybe I'm the lucky one after all,' she tried to tell herself.

What did Annette have in her life that she didn't? The kids, of course, was the obvious answer, but Margaret felt that she had enjoyed her nephew Fred over the years more than Annette had her kids, all that worry about what elementary school they should attend, and now they were both odious creatures who no one wanted to be around. Edward was absolutely afraid of them. And then, of course, Annette had Edward. But didn't Margaret have more of him, at least more of his time and kindness? 'Yes, I am much better off than Annette, and I even have my job. All she has is her exercise class and that friend of hers with the layered perm. I'd take Nel and her moods over that woman any day.' But it was still impossible to feel truly superior to Annette, try as she might. Maybe she was happier with her life, but there was something about Annette that let her reign supreme over everyone else. She was always right about everything, and no one would ever think of contradicting her about anything. And even Nel, for the most part, was only able to ignore her a bit.

Edward was the same as he'd always been, Margaret decided as she read the instructions in the cookbook again. Except for his obsession with his clothes, he was never in the present, something that Margaret had first attributed to his being mysterious and romantic. But after knowing him for a few years, she realized that he was constantly preoccupied with one abstract thing or another, and not at all concerned with the day to day problems of life, unless it involved his appearance. This realization, except for his vanity, had actually endeared him to her since she was easily able to help him with his preoccupations.

It wasn't up to her to worry about his day-to-day needs, she decided assertively as she turned on the water and tried to wash the sticky flour and butter from her hands. She was free to indulge him in his other concerns, like his work. But her hands weren't coming clean, so something more was needed. She reached cautiously for the heavy-duty cleaner that was kept under the sink. She was apprehensive because she always had the idea that large spiders lived under there even though she had never really seen one. Still, fear of the unknown had usually kept her away.

Thinking back to Edward, she remembered that he did seem too needy lately, especially for moral support. But it was probably just because he had married someone like Annette that he needed the closeness of his friends more. Annette seemed so cold and distant. No matter what the cause, though, his recent insecurities had become unattractive. On the other hand, his friends were probably the only personal contact in his life; he certainly didn't get that from his children. But she wasn't used to thinking about him in this pitiful kind of way, he was starting to seem almost pathetic.

'Wrap in waxed paper and chill for two hours...' After she was done washing her hands (she would put the cleaner back later), she scraped the dough into a ball, wrapped it in waxed paper, and put it into the refrigerator.

It was just as well she had stuck to the recipe since Edward and Annette would both be there. She didn't want Annette making any comments about her cooking. There would be six people, counting Annette's brother Tim. The pie would be big enough, and blueberry would go well with the salmon that Matt hoped to catch. Of course if he didn't catch anything, Nel would probably ask her to bring something else. She could always make a ham loaf; it was a good summertime dish and fairly easy. She got out her recipe file and began to read the ingredients, but then she remembered that horrible picnic about five or six years ago when Annette had asked, in front of several people, if it was spam. She quickly put the card back into the box; she could worry later about what to bring if Matt didn't catch a fish. He would probably catch something, he usually did.

CHAPTER XIV

Everyone stood around the fish gleefully admiring its obvious freshness. It had just been caught and was in perfect condition. Even the head was intact. Margaret looked at its eyes to see if they were any different from the eyes of the fish she bought at the supermarket. She had always heard that very fresh fish had a certain look in their eyes, but they had always looked the same to her. She'd have to ask Matt about that sometime when they were alone.

Someone would have to start cleaning it soon, and she hoped they would take it outside to do it. The cats should be seen to, she thought as she glanced around the room; but, of course, they were hiding with all these people around. She looked at the fish more closely. It certainly did seem fresh, almost alive: its eyes were clear and engaging. Wasn't it really more of a tragedy to kill a wild salmon like this one than some stupid chicken or cow that was raised to be slaughtered? Why did everyone think it was more acceptable even kind of cool, to kill and eat the salmon? The way salmon could find, even after several years out in the ocean, the same stream where they had been born and use every bit of their energy, to swim up that stream and lay their eggs, was infinitely more impressive than anything a chicken had ever done. She remembered a comment Louise had once made about salmon: 'I think it's horrible that those salmon are allowed to just swim upstream and die; someone should do something to help them!' Margaret smiled to herself as she bent down for a closer look.

As she leaned over, the fish tail flipped up and snapped back down onto the counter in such a forceful way that it sailed high into the air and then onto the floor where it landed on Margaret's foot. Everyone jumped back, startled by this sudden display of wildlife. Margaret looked down to see it flopping around on her top of her sandal. Since she was only wearing her old Dr. Scholl's, her toes were left unprotected and had become smeared by fish slime. Annette started to laugh. For a second, Margaret didn't know what to do. Everyone seemed to be staring at her feet. She lifted her skirt up to see the fish better; she could feel the slime between her toes. These probably weren't the best shoes to wear, but they seemed fine when she had looked in the mirror at home, they were hidden under her long silk paisley skirt and after all, it was just a potluck. The idea that a fish might jump on her feet had never occurred to her. She gently kicked it off and bent over to lay a dishtowel across her toes. She was blotting her feet when the fish flipped up once more, this time catching her nose. Everyone was startled again, and attention was diverted from Margaret's toes to her nose, which began to bleed immediately.

"Good god almighty," Matt's voice rang out in his most musical, southern drawl as he handed her another dishtowel.

It did seem like such an appropriate thing to say, and really the right way to say it. Annette put her hand over her mouth and turned away, Margaret heard her giggling as she ran from the room.

"Are you okay?" Tim, Annette's brother, put his arm around her shoulder. She noticed how tan and soft his neck looked. But his serious and concerned manner seemed out of place to her in such a comical situation.

Margaret started to giggle. "Of course. I'm fine. It's really so funny." But she didn't care much for Annette's stifled laughter; there was certainly no need to run from the room like a foolish teenager. And this overly concerned bedside manner on the part of her younger brother was irritating also. Of course, he was just trying to be nice but it wasn't as if she had done anything embarrassing or had a severe injury. Why, he was even rubbing her arm up and down as if she was losing body heat. Next thing I know, he'll probably offer me a blanket. She looked out from the towel that Tim was holding to her nose to see that Matt was scooping the fish off the floor with another towel. Edward was standing a safe distance away, eyeing the fish suspiciously; no doubt he was worried about his trousers. Then she caught Nel's eye and the two of them started to giggle. Pretty soon they were both laughing quite uncontrollably and couldn't stop. Then everyone else joined in, but after a few minutes the others had had enough. Margaret and Nel laughed on, though, until tears rolled down their cheeks.

They recovered themselves to find that everyone else had gone outside to clean the fish, except for Annette, who was standing in the kitchen looking at them quizzically.

She took a sip from the glass of white wine she was holding in her hand. "Are you two finished?"

They looked at each other and began to roar again. Margaret's stomach was beginning to ache, and her facial muscles were getting sore. She could feel the wrinkles setting in but every time she looked at Annette with her scornful air and then looked back to Nel, she started to laugh again. Finally Annette left the room and they were able to gain some control over themselves.

By the time they moved into the dining room, Margaret had recovered from any minor feelings of embarrassment she may have had about the fish and about laughing so hard. Except for Tim, she knew them all too well, and it was hard to be embarrassed about anything she did with Nel.

Nel always had so much self-confidence; she could get away with anything. Margaret reflected on how lucky she was to have Nel for a friend. What a blessing not to have her life filled with people like Annette, how depressing that would be. Sometimes she wondered why Nel had stayed friends with a spinster from Lakeview who lived in her mother's house, but it was easy to see that they always had fun together and agreed on so many things.

When Margaret took her seat at the table, she noticed that her view of Tim, who was sitting across from her, was obstructed by a vase of unsightly mums that were dyed an odd shade of pink.

"Do you mind if I move these?" Nel looked at Annette and then reached over to pick up the vase. Without waiting for an answer, she placed them on a table in the corner of the room. So that was Annette's contribution to the party. With all the flowers she had in her garden, why had she bought those?

As she waited for the food to be passed around, Margaret began to watch Annette. She hadn't been to Nel and Matt's in a long time, and she was busy surveying her surroundings. The amount of artwork in the room had increased a great deal since Annette had been there. A large wooden arm with several old rusty syringes hanging from it was mounted on a wheel that spun around, its title could be plainly seen, 'The Wheel of Misfortune.' Margaret was surprised to see Annette stand up and give it a whirl. Next she moved over to look at the TV which occupied a prominent place in the living room, a mortal sin in itself in Lakeview but here it was enshrined with candles and icons, and an imposing statue of the Virgin Mary stood on top of the set.

None of this was like anything you would see in Lakeview. Of course, Annette's house had lots of art, but somehow she had made sure that it wasn't too unusual, and the colors in the paintings even matched the palette of the rooms. There were no sculptures in Annette's house, only a few glass objects of ugly, oversized shells in horrid pastel colors. There was always an oversupply of that type of glass work at all the auctions; you could hardly even call it art.

Margaret's house, on the other hand, was really the same as it had been when her mother died. The antiques and Persian rugs had looked so natural that there didn't seem to be any reason to change them. Margaret had replaced the beige drapes with some nice chintz ones and re-covered a chair, but nothing else seemed necessary. The walls had filled up easily with paintings her friends had given her, and Matt's sculptures occupied any remaining spaces around the room.

Her thoughts were drawn back to the dinner party. Everyone was seated and had something on their plates, so it should have been a time for conversation, but no one was talking.

"We'll have to keep a look-out for Pablo's review of the art show. It might be in the paper soon." She tried to introduce a topic that had significance for so many of them, but no one was interested.

After a few minutes, Matt paused in his eating long enough to say, "Joan better watch out for Pablo, he's up to something." But Margaret didn't want to have a discussion about Joan and Pablo. She was relieved when Tim quickly asked a question about the museum, but then Annette immediately said she couldn't possibly sit there and listen to another conversation about 'that museum.' Things were quiet again until Margaret turned to Tim and began asking him the obligatory questions about his career.

She felt relieved when everyone else joined in and things finally took off.

"I'll be with a group that's out of First Hill Hospital," he was saying when Nel interrupted him.

"Isn't that where they took that guy who claimed he was an alien? He even had some of the doctors convinced. Remember? It made *The Enquirer*."

"Oh, I remember that! He had some strange body odor." Tim looked towards Annette, who had a cynical look on her face. "It was in our local papers, too," he added defensively.

"Have you seen the latest issue?" Nel was asking everyone. Margaret had noticed it at the check-out line, but she hesitated to speak up. "It has this great article about a dentist in Arizona who does all his work with his feet; he doesn't have any hands. It even has pictures."

"Oh, please." Annette looked away from the table and rolled her eyes.

"No, really, it's true. They document all their stories." Nel defended the publication as she smiled coyly at Annette. Margaret could see that Nel was having fun harassing her. It was entertaining to see Annette get all worked up. She was out of her element here, and was fair game.

"People do amazing things with their feet," Margaret offered, remembering the salmon. "Maybe I should have tried to flip that salmon back up to the counter with my foot." She held her fork out over her plate. It was piled high with a bite of the fresh, pink fish. "Or should I say, 'this salmon'?" She put the big bite into her mouth and smiled.

"You should have." Nel suddenly pushed herself away from the table and was trying to lift her foot up for everyone to see. "Hey, maybe we should all try eating with our feet. We could put our forks between our toes and try it."

"But our pants would get all wrinkled," Edward cautioned as everyone laughed. It was nice to know he could still make fun of himself.

"I don't think I could get my foot up on the table anymore," Matt said, "if I ever could."

"You could, Annette; you're in such great shape." Nel smiled at her in a disarmingly kind way. Annette looked back suspiciously but said nothing.

Margaret squirmed in her seat. She could feel that everyone was suddenly uncomfortable. "Where will you be living, Tim?"

He perked up again and began to answer, but Annette interrupted him before he could speak. "He'll be staying with us."

"Until they kick me out. I'll be living close to you, Margaret," he added in a rather bright way that seemed to call for an answer.

"Great." Margaret felt a little foolish. She put her fork down and looked around the table. Everyone seemed to be moving their eyes from Tim to her. Their eyebrows were all arched and they had surprised looks on their faces.

"Maybe you could show me around the neighborhood a bit?"

"I don't know what there is to show." Annette broke into the conversation once again. Her domineering tone startled Margaret. "You did, after all, grow up there, and it's not as if you never came back to visit."

Nel straightened in her chair and glared at Annette. "But he's probably lost touch with most people, except for Matt. He needs to get re-acquainted. Who better to do it than Margaret?"

"You'll definitely have to look after us when Annette goes to Spain in November." Edward confidently, almost bravely entered into the discussion.

Margaret was a little taken aback. All this arguing over two people becoming friends, and what was Edward insinuating? Was this what she had come to, a lonely spinster left to look after abandoned men? After all, this was the Nineties. They couldn't really think she had nothing better to do. Of course if Annette was going away, it would be a golden opportunity to have Edward over, and Tim was nice enough.

She began to imagine a cozy family-style meal with herself, Helen, Tim, and Edward on a cool November evening with a pleasant drizzle coming down. They could have a snug fire and relax in the living room.

"He'll be too busy anyway." Annette put her final stamp on everything. She flashed Margaret a superior look as if the whole thing had been Margaret's idea and she had put a stop to it.

Margaret felt she would like to change the subject again, but she'd changed it so much before that she was tired of trying to soothe things over. This was obviously not a very agreeable group of people for a dinner party. Probably it was unpleasant because there were six of them. Wasn't there some little quotation her mother always used to say? 'Six a poor mix, eight is always great.'

After dinner, Margaret helped Tim clear the dishes. As she moved around the table, she could hear Annette whispering sharply to Edward in the living room; she was obviously anxious to leave. Margaret was able to make out several reasons why Annette felt they needed to go immediately. But it seemed to her that both Tim and Edward wanted to stay a while longer; she waited to see if either of them would confront Annette. It didn't surprise her when neither of them did. There was another uncomfortable air about the party and by the time the three of them left, it felt like a relief.

"What a stupid evening," Nel was saying as she bent over to load the dishwasher. "I should never have let Matt talk me into this; it's all his fault. Annette is such a bitch; she's intolerable. I don't see how Eddie can stand it. Ha!" she laughed, "it's a good thing he's such an imbecile." Margaret smiled: this was Nel at her best, raking everyone over the coals.

"I should make her pay for ruining my evening. I know, I'll ask her to have an Avon party for me! All those hard-body women wear tons of makeup."

"What was all that talk about Africa and Avon anyway?" Margaret called out from the dining room where she was clearing the table.

"Africa and Avon? What are you talking about?"

"Matt said that your selling Avon had to do with the Woodabe Tribe in Africa."

"Are you talking about me?" he shouted from the backyard, where he was scraping the grill.

"Oh, that. Well, you know how Matt is; he thought I might have some sort of ideological problem selling Avon. So I told him that it was a socio-cultural thing, and that every society and culture had adorned their bodies. It's true, you know. In the Woodabe tribe, the men wear the makeup."

"I bet some of those male body-builders wear makeup. Have Annette invite them to the party."

"I have to admit, I did enjoy making fun of that body of hers. She must spend at least three hours a day on it. What a waste of time. It's a mindless existence, and she didn't eat anything." She paused, turning the water off, and then looked around towards Margaret. "Her boobs were never that big."

Margaret froze. She was on her way back from the dining room and had a large tray of dirty dishes suspended in front of her. "No, they weren't. She's thinner, but her boobs have gotten bigger."

"Nobody could be that skinny and have breasts like that." Water dripped from Nel's hands onto the floor.

Margaret had to sit down. "I can't believe it." She shook her head back and forth and gazed off into space.

"Do you believe it?" Nel's open mouth broke into a big grin, and she started to laugh. "She's had a boob job. She's actually had her breasts done! Hey, you know what? I bet Eddie hasn't even figured it out yet."

CHAPTER XV

Helen fussed around the living room straightening the pillows on the chairs. "What time did they say they'd be over?" she asked Margaret for the third time.

"Elaine, Elaine," Margaret was repeating out loud over and over as she ground the decaffeinated coffee beans: she wanted to make sure she didn't call Elaine 'Susan' by mistake. She had decided on decaffeinated coffee for Helen's sake, since she couldn't have her getting too excited.

"Fred said they'd be here around five o'clock. Now you know they will only be here for a few minutes. They have some dinner plans, and then they're going to a concert."

"I know, I know." Helen kicked the ottoman over to the side of the room. "I'm not a moron."

Margaret ignored Helen's remark as she walked into the living room to check things. "Shouldn't we sit out on the deck? I probably should have made iced tea instead of coffee, it's so hot." But the door bell was ringing.

"Too late now." Helen walked to the door.

Although Margaret knew that Elaine looked like Susan, she was not prepared for the initial shock of seeing her. Like Susan, she was thin and boyish-looking with short blond hair. She also had a strong jaw and rather sharp features like Susan's. But it wasn't just her physical traits that startled her: she even dressed the same, and even though it was boiling out, she had on a loose, baggy, dark gray suit that hung off her shoulders, just like something Susan would have worn.

Helen was left standing at the door with an astonished look on her face while Margaret, who was able to collect herself faster, directed them out to the deck.

"Would you like decaf coffee or iced tea?" Margaret immediately felt that she sounded too formal and stiff.

"Iced tea would be fine," Elaine answered and Fred nodded.

Helen joined Margaret in the kitchen, where she began to prepare the tea. "If it's decaf, I'll have the tea." She peered into the pot.

"Well, they're both decaf."

"Oh, all right then." Helen slammed down the lid of the coffee pot. "I don't see why you waste money on that decaf. I just don't get the point of it."

Margaret spooned the tea into the water. "She looks just like Susan, doesn't she?"

"'Happiness was born a twin,'" Helen quoted in a whisper. "She's even dressed like her, and did you notice? No jewelry or makeup, just like Susan."

They put the ice in the glasses and poured Margaret's coffee.

"Well, it's certainly a beautiful day." Another stiff remark on her part, Margaret thought as she carried out the tray. "Summer is finally here." She sat the drinks down and looked up to see Helen gawking at Elaine. "Here's your tea, Susan."

Elaine hesitated before she took the glass. "It's Elaine," she said simply, and of course Margaret had known that as soon as she had said it. So much for repeating her name over and over all afternoon. She had been sure that Helen would be the first to make that mistake, but no, it had to be her. The resemblance was just so uncanny, which probably made her mistake even more embarrassing. She could feel it becoming a big issue that would probably never be discussed openly, but left there to smolder beneath the surface. She couldn't imagine anyone bringing up the subject in conversation, except maybe Helen, and what a disaster that would be.

It could even be that Fred hadn't realized how much she looked like Susan. Of course, there was the hope that they would stop seeing each other, and that would be the end of that problem. Margaret felt a little guilty hoping for that, though. Much better to wish that they live happily ever after, she told herself.

"I'm sorry, habit I guess." She tried to busy herself with her cup and saucer. "Have you been out enjoying the weather?"

Fred took a sip of his tea. "Yes, we had a great day at Hawthorn Beach."

"Isn't that the gay beach?" Helen blurted out.

Fred looked at Elaine and smiled. "Well, yes, but I think a lot of different kinds of people go there. It's a neighborhood beach."

"That's just great, as it should be," Margaret faltered. Perhaps she shouldn't be defending gay people to Fred; after all he had been terribly hurt by Susan's running away. But really, Helen should know better than to make such a comment at a time like this.

"I'm so glad you came by." Helen turned to Fred, her voice was suddenly very serious. "I want to know what you think of this quotation: 'They made her a grave, too cold and damp for a soul so warm and true.' Helen's words hung in the air for several seconds as everyone considered them.

"But the 'they' would mean us, wouldn't it? I mean, it would be the people who buried her. Like you, Aunt Helen."

"Oh! I hadn't thought about that." She was suddenly flustered.

Margaret noticed that Elaine didn't seem very puzzled by this odd conversation. She could imagine Fred filling her in before he brought her over, 'my slightly crazy spinster aunts.' It was probably better to prepare her ahead of time, to break her in gently.

"What restaurant are you going to tonight?" Margaret was happy to be able to come up with another topic of conversation.

"We're going to an Italian place over by the Palladium, and then we're going to see The Real Women." Fred looked at Elaine and smiled. "It's Elaine favorite group." Margaret had heard of the well-known lesbian band; she was hoping that Helen had not. She tried to catch her eye, but

Helen was staring at Elaine's shoes. They were very interesting, like cowboy boots that had been cropped off at the ankle. Margaret thought they might look nice with the new brown cords she had just bought at the Anniversary Sale at Nordstrom's.

During the silence, Margaret looked at her watch and tried to think of something else to talk about; it seemed too nosy to ask her what kind of work she did. Then watching Elaine gaze into Fred's eyes, Margaret was struck by how much she must adore him. They had been dating six weeks now and were certainly still excited about each other; perhaps she was the one for him after all. Fred certainly didn't seem to be content without a mate. He must really need to be with someone, maybe because he was an only child. He was probably always lonely, she thought a little sadly.

"Let me show you the pond," he was saying. "I had so much fun back here as a kid." They both stood up and walked towards the small pond that was hidden in a corner of the yard. As she sat on the deck and watched them, Margaret let her thoughts drift back to her college days when she and Edward first began dating, to those feelings of adoring passion and unsettling obsession. But being in love wasn't a very pleasant situation, if one really thought about it. The lack of self-control and all that uncertainty about what might happen was unnerving. Edward, and her feelings for him, had absolutely taken over her mind, even though they had dated for only nine months. It wasn't until after she had stopped thinking about him so much that she was able to look back and see just how much their relationship had consumed her. Of course, the breakup was the hardest time, and then it had taken her about a year to stop obsessing about him. After that she was able to go on with her life.

It wasn't until about ten years later, after all the usual boring dates and disappointments, after she had given up any hope of marrying at all, that she decided that maybe they still had a relationship: a relationship which was possibly even better than if they had gotten married in the first place.

But now, as she thought back over the last few months to the way he had treated her during their little board squabble, the way he had pouted and groveled, he seemed almost pitiful. She was beginning to realize how unpleasant marrying Edward could have been. True, he was still very good looking but there was no getting away from his shallowness.

Perhaps she had never wanted to marry him, or anyone else, in the first place, and being in love with him had offered her the opportunity to avoid thinking about marriage... those instincts that every red-blooded woman or man was supposed to have. It was a relief, in fact, not to have them controlling you. She leaned back into her Adirondack chair feeling content and relaxed.

Helen's laughter came from across the lawn; in her straightforward, eccentric way she had apparently broken the ice with Elaine.

"I'll never forget, once when Fred was about two or three, he came back here and just disappeared. Of course, we had drained the pond as soon as he started to crawl and didn't fill it up again until he was seven. But anyway, I called him and called him, but he didn't answer. Finally, I found him under a rhododendron bush, just sitting there, staring at a bug. He loved it back here. Oh, Fred, you were just so cute then." Helen poked him in the ribs. "He's still cute, don't you think, Elaine."

"Yes, definitely." She laughed.

"Aunt Margaret," Fred called out playfully. "What about you? Do you think I'm still cute?"

"No doubt about it." She walked over to join them. "It's unanimous: We all think you're cute. And, of course, we're totally unbiased in our opinion."

"Of course. It's just so much fun to be cute," he put his arm around Elaine, and they both laughed. "Listen, Aunties, it's been great, but we gotta go."

They walked around the side of the house to leave, arms around each other. How good it felt to see Fred so happy again. May he always be so happy, she thought to herself as she watched them walk up the hill to his car. Please, just don't let her find out that she's gay.

ello." Louise answered her phone with a feeling of excitement that quickly changed to indifference when she realized it was only her socially needy friend, Colleen.

"Louise?" Colleen said, in a conspiratory whisper. "I just walked by the Philbrick's, and they're pruning their tree."

"Oh, my god! Okay, 'bye." Louise slammed the telephone down in Colleen's ear and ran quickly upstairs to have a look out the bedroom window.

Sure enough, Tex and a younger man who was obviously his assistant could be seen unloading equipment from Tex's truck. Renee, Margaret, and Denise were just entering the house; Louise quickly determined that they must be there for a meeting about the stupid Octoberfest. Well, at least Joan wouldn't be able to interfere with her plans with Tex if she was being kept busy by a silly meeting.

She looked around her bedroom. The bed wasn't made since Terry and Betty were due to come that day... how irritating to have them scheduled every time Tex was around. Oh well, she would just have to throw the bedspread over it.

In a panic, she changed clothes and touched up her makeup. Maybe a little flirting might help things along. "No harm in trying," she decided as she reached to the back of her makeup drawer for a redder shade of lipstick than she usually wore. Then she checked her purse to see how much money she had, she counted a hundred and fifty dollars; plenty of money. That settled she rushed down the stairs of her house and crossed the street. She was relieved to see that Tex was standing on the street side of the laurel hedge so they would be free to conspire without Joan seeing them through her window. He had a long rope thrown over his shoulder: A good sign, Louise decided as she stepped onto the sidewalk. A rope meant he was planning to climb the tree.

"Hello, Tex, how are you?" Louise smiled and put forth her sweetest voice. "I'm so sorry I missed you when you came back to prune our Japanese maple. I thought you were planning to come a week later, but you came the next day."

"Oh, hello, Louise. How's it going?" He was surprised to see her again; he'd forgotten that she lived across the street from the Philbricks. She was looking pretty good, better than he remembered, not so dowdy.

"Do you remember that other little business we were talking about the last time I saw you? Do you think you could sneak upstairs with me for just a minute right now and I could explain what I need again? It wouldn't take long at all, and since you haven't started working yet, this would be an ideal time. I guess you could almost say that it's now or never, I've waited so long," she giggled.

He looked around nervously to see where his assistant, Jason, was. Thank goodness she was at least whispering. This woman was amazingly persistent: he'd had women come on to him at work before but never like this. Well, she had said she was desperate. How long had it been for her, he tried to remember, four years was it? And why did she want the whole thing to be so quick? She must really like to get down to it.

"So you're still thinking about us doing that, are you, Louise?" he leaned over and whispered in her ear.

"Oh, yes!" She smiled and gazed up into his eyes.

Tex walked over to Jason and gave him a few instructions about the hedge, then he followed her across the street and up the back stairs to her house. He could hear the women in Joan's backyard laughing; he would have to be quick if he didn't want Mrs. Philbrick to walk out and find him gone. Of course he could always say Louise had some work for him to look at, which was true since he had worked for her before.

"They must be having their meeting," she said as they walked up the stairs.

"The ladies? Yep, they must be cookin' up something." He glanced back towards Joan's house with an uncomfortable feeling of embarrassment as soon as he spoke. They were the ones who were cookin' up something, if anybody was.

"That's right. We're having a little Octoberfest here in a few of weeks: lederhosen, an oompa band, and all that."

"You are? I'll have to give her one of my cards; it's probably been years since I gave her one. Do you think they've hired the caller yet? What's the name of the band?"

"I don't think you have a caller for an Octoberfest, do you? Isn't that for square dances?"

He put his hand on her shoulder as they walked into the house. "You gotta have a caller, honey. Who do you think is gonna get everybody out on the dance floor?"

Louise was a little startled by his friendly manner, calling her 'honey' and touching her shoulder; it seemed a little too familiar, even for two conspirators. "My husband," she tried to enunciate her words in a pointed way, "will be so glad to hear that you're taking care of this for us. He thinks I'm going to extremes. He doesn't know how much I need this."

"Your husband!" He stopped abruptly and was staring at her with a shocked look on his face. "Does he know about this?"

"Oh, he didn't want me to prune the Japanese maple, but this is different, he approves of this completely. What we're doing now is nothing compared to some of the ideas I've had. He was afraid I'd end up in jail before the whole thing was over. I told you, I'm absolutely desperate. It'll be fine; they'll never know. You're perfect for the job; you're such an artist with the pruning shears. Now here's a hundred dollars for your trouble."

"A hundred dollars? I don't take money for doing this!"

"Oh, I know you don't usually do this type of thing, but I'd feel so much better if you took this. I know I'll get my money's worth."

Tex put his hand on his head and tried to collect his thoughts. 'Desperate' wasn't the word to describe this woman. 'And how does jail figure into this? What was she getting at?' he wondered as he tried to put the odd pieces of this puzzle together. It seemed like every time he got with this woman, something wasn't right.

Her husband approved; now that was strange right there. And she was so determined to get what she wanted, she was even going to end up in jail over this. 'They would never know,' who were 'they'? And why was this the ideal time, why did it have to be now?

Suddenly it hit him like a ton of drywall, and he realized what she had been talking about all this time. Thank god he had caught himself before he had gotten into some real trouble. This was not something a responsible man should do without thinking over first, and very carefully, too. There were real repercussions to consider, repercussions that would last a lifetime.

He looked down at her. There she stood with the money in her hand; he would have to put her off yet be careful not to insult her. Sure, he felt sorry for her, it was easy to see that she was getting old and her clock was ticking, but he also had an overwhelming urge to get out of there, and fast.

"Louise, I'm very flattered that you're asking me to do this for you. I know how important it must be to you, how much you must want this, but I just... I just need to think it over."

"You can't think it over," she blurted out. "This is our only chance; it could be two years."

"Now I know there are certain times that are better than others," he started to slowly back up towards the door, "but I just have to think it over. I'll give you a call." Then he quickly turned and ran down the back steps and out the gate before she could speak.

Once he got down to the sidewalk, he stopped running. He felt as if he'd just narrowly escaped from some kind of grave danger. As he stood there a minute, feeling shaky, the sounds of women's voices came to him between the buzz of Jason's pruning shears. For a second, he thought he might faint.

"Are you all right?" a woman was asking him. "Did you have an accident?" She turned to look up into the tree.

"He did not fall out of the tree, Terry. He's standing up."

"Well, you look faint. Why don't you sit down? Betty, go get Joan." The woman gently pushed him down so that he was sitting on the curb.

"No, I'm fine," he tried to insist but one of them left anyway. She was back almost instantly with three other women. Now there were five of them standing over him. He could hear Jason saying, "He couldn't have fallen out of a tree; he wasn't even up a tree!"

"Shouldn't he be wearing a harness?"

"I'm telling you, ma'am, he wasn't up a tree!"

"It's this heat. Why, it hasn't rained for at least two weeks, and it must be seventy-eight degrees out right now."

"And it's not even noon; any one of us could pass out any second. Maybe we should call Bill at the hospital."

"Hold it, hold it!" Tex stood up with his hands in the air. He was starting to feel much better, and he certainly wasn't going to any hospital. "I'm fine, really, I'm okay. I just need to get back to my prunin', and I'll be all right." He picked up his shears and began to work on the hedge. "What are you lookin' at?" he snapped to Jason.

"Nothin'."

"Oh shoot, that reminds me." He reached into his pocket and pulled out his wallet. "Mrs. Philbrick," he called out to Joan as she walked towards the house. "I understand you ladies are planning an Octoberfest. I want you to have my card. Have you booked a caller yet?"

"A caller? What does a caller do at an Octoberfest?"

"Well," Tex smiled as he sauntered up to her, "I know what I'd do, I'd have you all dancin' before you know it. There's lots of German dances you can do; a caller can really get things goin'. Who's your band?"

"The Bavarian Oompah Band. They were able to give us a great deal. But I don't think we could afford a caller. It might be nice though... what do you normally charge?"

"That's a great band; I've worked with them before. I could give you three hours for about seventy-five dollars."

"Seventy-five dollars! That's a lot. What do you charge people who are fund-raising for The Children's Homeless Guild, who have no money?"

"Now that's a tough one, but I got to eat, you know. I gotta make a living wage."

"Well, I don't want you to stop eating," she smiled. "But you could write off the difference on your taxes. Come on, give me a real offer, something I can work with. Those other women will have a fit if I walk back into this meeting with another seventy-five dollar expense."

"Okay, we'll make it fifty." Tex took off his hat and wiped his brow. "It's a good thing you don't try to get my pruning estimate down too much; I wouldn't have a roof over my head if you did."

"Speaking of your head, I think you should skip pruning the deodara today. I don't want you getting dizzy and falling out of my tree. When you're done with the hedge," she ordered, "come inside and I'll write up a short contract for the Octoberfest with the time and date." As she walked towards the house, she turned around to face him with her finger pointing at his chest. "Three hours for fifty dollars, right?"

"That's right, Mrs. Philbrick," he answered sheepishly. "Three hours for fifty dollars."

Tex walked back towards the hedge, the sound of the pruning shears was reassuring to him after all this business with these women. He was relieved to have a day of hard work ahead of him.

CHAPTER XVII

*L*ouise divided the next two hours between sitting on her deck and looking out from her upstairs bedroom window. She still had the faintest hope they might cut just the right limb to increase her view; after all, the tree hadn't been pruned at all last year so they were sure to cut some of it now. They had never gone more than two years without pruning it at least a little. She watched intently as Tex and the boy worked on the laurel hedge, the boy on the ladder doing the top and Tex clipping the sides and picking up the debris.

Finally, after over two hours, they were done with the front hedge. They moved to the backyard to cut that side of the lot. With Tex back there pruning, she expected to see the meeting break up since there was no way they would be able to hear each other with those electric clippers going. Sure enough, after only a few minutes, she could hear women's voices as the four moved their meeting into the house.

Louise was beginning to regret that she was 'out of the loop' with the Octoberfest; it wasn't like her to be left out of a big guild function like this one. Of course, Joan had retained control over everything by not opening up the work to the guild members in general. Instead she had hand picked a few of her best friends to do everything, which was certainly not in the true spirit of the guild and shouldn't be tolerated.

She may not get the tree pruned this year, Louise resolved, but at least she would try and figure out something to do about this Octoberfest. Hoping she might catch some last-minute details when the women left, Louise moved down to the spot behind her fence that was closest to Joan's front door. An old stump was conveniently placed where she could sit down, and there was even a small opening in the railings of the fence that she could peep through. Her neck felt stiff, and it was a relief not to have to strain her head outwards the way she had done all morning. She slumped down and started to rub her temples. Looking at her watch she calculated that she had spent over two hours watching and waiting for Tex to prune the tree and Joan to end her meeting. What a waste of her time.

Thinking back on what had happened that day, Louise began to wonder why Tex had been so terrified at the idea of going behind Joan's back, and just to do a little pruning. One or two branches of that massive tree would make no difference whatsoever to Joan. The galling thought that he might be concerned about being hired as the caller for that stupid dance began to grate on her. After all, he was willing enough to do the work before she told him about the dance. The more she thought about it, the more obvious it became to her that there could be no other possible explanation; it certainly couldn't be because of the money, that was for sure.

Her head began to ache at the thought of Joan and her silly dance, and all the trouble it had caused her. It wasn't fair that Joan could always get the guild to go along with anything she wanted, just because her husband was a doctor and they had so much money.

And how sneaky of Joan to wait until she and Colleen were out of town so she could push the whole thing through behind their backs; croquet and Mozart would have been much more refined. Drinking beer just didn't fit in with the image the guild should be portraying to the world. Well, she and Colleen would just be too busy that night, she decided. They couldn't possibly make it to a silly beer-drinking fiasco.

Suddenly it dawned on Louise that most people didn't even know the date of the Octoberfest yet, and that if she could plan a dinner party for that night and get people to commit to it now, there would be no way they could back out later. She toyed with the idea of having a large cocktail party, but it might cause too much talk and she could look bad. No, it was much better to have a smaller party with a few key people, ten at the most. She decided that the best plan of attack would be to invite people from the other guild in the neighborhood;

they wouldn't feel obligated to show up to support the dance since they were in the other guild.

Of course, Colleen would not be invited to the dinner party; she could just stay home and that would enable Louise to add two more people to the boycott list. Feeling inspired by her new idea, she decided to go into the house so she could call Colleen and make out her guest list. Standing up, Louise lifted her head just in time to catch Terry's eye as she walked out of Joan's house with her cleaning supplies. Her bucket flew into the air as Terry jumped back in surprise.

"Louise, what on Earth are you doing hiding behind the fence?"

"Oh, just a little weeding." That silly woman, how dare she accuse her of hiding behind her own fence? She bent over to yank up a clump of baby's-breath so she would have something to wave in her hand. "See you in a few minutes," she called out in her sweetest voice and then, throwing the baby's-breath down, she stormed into her house.

Since the steps up to Louise's backyard were too steep to navigate with cleaning supplies, Terry and Betty always loaded up their gear and drove around from the front of Joan's house to the front of Louise's. By the time they arrived, Louise was waiting at the door to let them in.

"I've already cleaned the upstairs bathroom, so instead of doing that" Oh no, here we go, Terry thought to herself as she listened to Louise drivel on. "...would the two of you take out all the books in the library and dust off the shelves?"

Terry tightened her grip on the bucket she was holding. "I don't think we'll have time for that

An old stump was conveniently placed
where she could sit down, and there was even
a small opening in the railings of the fence
that she could peep through.

today." They had learned long ago to be assertive with Louise. "It's about time to give the walnut bed-set a coat of oil though; we'll do that instead. It'll take about the same amount of time as the bathroom would."

"Fine, but I want those bookshelves done sometime soon," Louise said sharply as she turned to go into the kitchen. Terry looked Betty and they both rolled their eyes.

"Do you want us to start upstairs or down?"

"Upstairs is fine."

Betty led the way up the stairs carrying the vacuum cleaner. She stopped in front of the bathroom door and looked inside. "Just like I thought, she hasn't done a thing in here."

"Well, we're not touching it." Terry switched on the vacuum in the hall just in time for them to hear Louise yelling, "Did you call me?"

"Ignore her," Betty whispered over the noise.

They finished the upstairs with Louise coming up to check on them only once, which was unusual. It was getting very hot, and Terry was in no mood for Louise, but when they came down the stairs to start on the first floor, she was waiting for them on the bottom step. Terry felt penned in since there was no reason for them to go back upstairs and Louise was holding her hand firmly on the railing, preventing them from going down any farther.

"How are things over at Joan's?" Louise cooed in a friendly manner. It wasn't the first time she had tried to get information out of them by being amiable. She usually offered some obvious tidbit of information hoping to get them to start talking, but years ago they had made a pact to tell her nothing.

"Fine. Just fine," Terry answered shortly without looking at her.

"I feel a little guilty I'm not over there helping them. I know they're working on the Octoberfest for our guild. I'll have to give her a call. I could bring some potato salad or something like that." Standing on the bottom stair, she leaned against the railing and crossed her arms; her foot dangled across the bottom step, closing off their escape.

"I wonder if they hired Tex to be the caller for the dance; he seems like so much fun," she went on, almost to herself.

"Oh, you mean the tree pruner." Betty used her shoulder to force her way past Louise. "We found him almost passed out on the front lawn."

"Passed out?" Louise actually was concerned. "I'll have to call her for sure now, to check on how he's doing. He does our pruning, too."

Terry felt irritated at Betty for telling Louise something that would get back to Joan, no matter how harmless it seemed. She wanted to catch her eye and give her a dirty look but Betty had escaped down the stairs and was moving into the living room. Although they told Joan everything, they didn't want her to think they ever repeated anything they heard at her house, especially to Louise.

"I'll offer to order the beer for the dance and check on Tex." Louise moved over to the phone.

"But he's fine now; he pruned their whole hedge today," Terry said quickly, trying to stop Louise from calling. "And Renee and Randal are arranging the beer."

"Oh, they are. Well..." she sighed. "I'll just have to think of something else to do." Terry was relieved when Louise seemed to give up on the idea of checking on Tex and went upstairs instead.

Louise smiled to herself as she walked up the stairs; she was suppressing a strong urge to cry out 'Eureka.' This was the information she needed, an absolute windfall. Renee and Randal were to arrange for the beer and wine, just as they had done for the guild's Christmas party, and since Louise, as the guild treasurer, had paid for everything, she knew exactly where they would order it. This was even better than if she had heard the news herself, because now no one knew that she knew. She could act with impunity, and she would tell no one about her plan, not even Colleen. It would be so much fun to ruin Joan's Octoberfest, and she would be saving the guild money because everyone would have bought their tickets ahead of time and the guild would not have to pay for their beer.

Of course now she would have to throw all her support behind the event; there would be no point in having the dinner party because she certainly couldn't miss seeing the look on Joan's face when, right at the beginning of the dance, in front of everyone, she realized there would be no beer at her party. Joan would look like such a fool, and everyone would think that she hadn't planned things well enough.

As she moved around the upstairs to check Terry and Betty's cleaning, Louise began to calculate when the best time would be to cancel the beer. It would be better to wait until the last minute so that if Renee called to confirm when the kegs would be delivered, it would be too late to reorder them. Louise stood looking out the bedroom window; the smell of lemon oil filled the room. She was so excited about her new plan that she wasn't even too despondent at the sight of Tex packing up his gear across the street. There would be no tree pruning again this year. Oh, well, she would have him back next spring after he had had a chance to think things over. Maybe he would still do the job for her. Besides, she told herself, summer was half over and that was when she enjoyed her view most. It didn't matter so much in the winter; the other trees lost all their leaves then anyway and her view got a little better for free. An Octoberfest without beer, she mused once again: Joan would never live this one down.

CHAPTER XVIII

Joan circled the block for the third time, trying once again to spot the entrance to the new underground parking garage beneath the university library. By then, she was driving rather fast and she cut off a pedestrian who was trying to cross the street that looped around the school.

"Oh, shut up," she hissed as the man yelled and shook his fist at her. Looking at her watch, she realized she was already ten minutes late and hadn't even found the parking garage yet. Then she finally saw it, a small tunnel without a sign in sight. "This is just what I get for standing around gossiping with Terry and Betty," she chided herself out loud. But she had heard some good stuff, she smiled as she remembered that Terry had called Colleen, 'a know-it-all who knows nothing.' It had sounded so profound coming from Terry, who never said an insulting word about anybody.

As she drove round and round the ramps, which took her farther down into the garage, she reflected on how odd it was that this was her old college campus. The cars were all clean and new, and the people were such a cross-section of ages, not at all like when she was in school. But then again, she didn't look like a student now either and, of course, neither would Pablo. She began to wonder if she would even recognize him; after all, it had been at least four years since she had last seen him. "When that friend of Fred's, what's his name, had the art opening," she mumbled as she finally pulled into a spot. But no, that wasn't right, he had come to their open house last Christmas.

But they hadn't really talked much that night; he had only asked about Margaret and said that he was getting remarried, which must have been his third since he had just been married for the second time when she first met him in graduate school. He had been rather flamboyant back then, a mid-thirties up-and-coming professor; he was not just a teachers assistant like so many of his contemporaries.

But that second wife... Joan tried to think as she walked across the campus towards the museum about what had happened with the second wife. The site of an elderly man with a briefcase walking on the lawn with an attractive young woman at his side reminded her: Pablo had married a cute young undergraduate, a freshman, who had gone on an art history tour he had conducted to Europe one summer. There had been quite a stir at the time, the girl's parents becoming involved as well as the administration, but she couldn't remember what else had happened. Try as she might, she couldn't recall any more except that the girl had come up to her one day after class and said some bizarre and inappropriate things about her marriage to Pablo. Joan stopped abruptly in the middle of the sidewalk and tried to remember what it was that Pablo's wife had said to her. She scolded herself, it wasn't like her to forget something so important. But then, it had been almost twenty years, she thought, as she started walking again.

Of course, today that kind of thing would be sexual harassment: a young girl barely over eighteen falling in love with a dazzling art history professor eighteen or more years her senior. There was often an element of worship involved between a student and teacher that didn't exist between employee and employer. She began to imagine a student eagerly awaiting the teacher's approval for some piece of artwork or an essay. They would be sitting in a dusty old office, full of miscellaneous clutter and books. Or, it could be a female professor with a young male student, but it was hard to imagine a young man waiting with bated breath for the approval of an elderly female English teacher.

She could picture, if she really strained her imagination, a chic art teacher impressing a young male art student, but her thoughts were interrupted by the sight of Pablo standing stiffly at the entrance of the museum. Although it was a warm sunny day, he was dressed entirely in black and carried an unopened umbrella in his hand that he moved around like a cane. He hadn't changed much in the last year, except for an amusing attempt to adapt a youthful, modern look with that silly ponytail. He seemed irritated and looked at his watch twice before he saw her. But when she reached the top of the stairs, he was all smiles as he took her elbow to lead her into the museum.

"I'm so sorry to be late; thank you for waiting." She tried to sound formal but apologetic.

"Did you have trouble parking?"

"Yes, but I can't really use that as an excuse," she laughed. "I started talking to my cleaning ladies and lost track of time."

"Cleaning ladies! You have cleaning ladies! I must have them!" he demanded with a smile on his face. "I'm desperate."

She looked at him cautiously; she had never referred any bachelors to Terry and Betty, of course he could still be married, but with his track record he was probably divorced again and kept a messy house. And he wouldn't be worried about keeping his place clean if he was married, that was for sure. On the other hand, maybe she should refer him. It would be so entertaining for Terry and Betty to find out about his single life. Of course, it was likely that he traveled a great deal; it could end up being easy money for them.

"I'd be happy to give them your number, but first things first. Let's look at all this beautiful art." Anyway, there was no point in giving him their number until he committed to what she wanted. There would be time to consider the options after he completed the article. "I'm just thrilled you've agreed to review our little art show; it's so nice to keep in touch this way. Of course, every one of our artists has been reviewed in the paper many times."

"I am truly desperate for someone to help me keep the place tidy. I only have a small apartment, but the view is fabulous. It would be easy for them to clean," he brought the subject back to Terry and Betty. But then his voice changed: "I'd love to show it to you sometime," he added in a lower tone.

"Oh, before I forget, I have two free tickets for you to a very special party. It's going to be so much fun; don't feel like you have to dress up."

She took two orange-colored tickets from her purse and handed them to him. He seemed at a loss as to what to do with them.

"An Octoberfest? Is it a Wagner celebration, The Ring?"

"The Ring? Oh, you mean the opera," she laughed. "No, this is just for fun. It's only a few blocks from here, just stop in."

With his hand on her elbow, Pablo stopped Joan in the museum foyer and whispered softly into her ear, "I would be thrilled."

And it was then that she remembered what his young wife had said to her twenty years ago, almost as confidentially as he was speaking now:

"Do you know what Pablo whispers to me when we're making love?" she had told her in a hall-way of the Art Building.

"He whispers 'Joan'."

At this point, one of the museum guards came up to tell them the museum was officially closed until the opening of the art show, but Joan composed herself and straightened things out so that they were allowed to begin their preview tour. Most of the exhibit was of glass art, but some paintings had been included to fill up the walls. Naturally, people were more apt to buy a painting for a few hundred dollars than an esoteric glass sculpture for thousands.

"I believe this lovely painting must be of you," he murmured as they stopped in front of a large oil on canvas.

"Of me?" Joan looked up to see one of Matt's more realistic paintings of a nude woman.

"Yes. I believe you know the artist, and I see the resemblance around the eyes and also in the shape of the breasts."

"The breasts?" she echoed in a curious tone as she dropped her purse, its contents spilling onto the floor. She quickly started to lean over to pick it up but then hesitated. She knew he would look down her blouse if she bent over.

Before she could make up her mind to squat down instead of lean, he said, "Yes, your breasts." His face was very close to hers, his chin was sticking out a bit and his eyes were half closed.

Although it had been a few years since this type of thing had happened to Joan, it wasn't the first time an obnoxious man had tried something with her, so she was quickly able to recover herself, retrieve the contents of her purse in a graceful way, and calculate her next move.

Of course, she decided, she would play along with him in a fun sort of way, make a joke of everything. He would have to write the article for the paper within the next few days; she could placate him for that long, and then there was always Terry and Betty. She could use them as a carrot for at least a week and then, once the article was published, refuse to give him their number. They would just be too busy, she resolved. She smiled as she thought about how the three of them would laugh over it all later. This would be a piece of cake, if only she hadn't already given him those two free tickets to the Octoberfest.

"You're flattering me, Pablo. My breasts are nothing like these at all. It's these padded bras, they work wonders. Now if I calculated this correctly, the review will have to go into next Friday's Arts Section of the paper in order to benefit our little event. Here's a list of all the things I want you to include in the article; I thought this might save you some time," she went on in a businesslike tone as she handed him an official-looking report. "It lists all the times, dates, artists, who the show benefits, and some prominent patrons' names are there, you know, to entice the social climbers. I really want everything included; I don't think you can leave anything out."

She took his elbow and steered him towards the museum door. She found herself thinking that these little needs of his were actually enabling her to assert some power over him. "And as far as Terry and Betty are concerned, I'd be happy to give them your number. You can't imagine how wonderful they are; they'll take care of everything for you. But, I'm sorry to say, they leave tomorrow for Oregon to help with their sick mother, so don't expect to hear from them for at least two weeks."

At the door, Pablo seemed to sputter out a few words like 'view', and 'my darling,' but she quickly interrupted him. Instead of responding to his mutterings, she turned to look him straight in the eye and demanded kindly and with a smile, "You do want Terry and Betty, don't you, Pablo?"

"Yes, naturally I want them, but it's you I need. I've always needed."

"Of course you need me, and I need you too. That's why we're here." Joan could feel a righteous power building in her veins, the power of someone who is on a mission to better humanity. She felt she was justified in doing whatever it took to reach her goal. "I think we should have lunch," she offered with a cozy smile. "I don't have my calendar with me now, but I'll call you and we'll set a date. Okay?"

"How about tomorrow?"

"Tomorrow might work; let me just check my calendar." As they walked down the stairs of the museum, she noticed classes had just let out and hundreds of students were hurrying across the campus in criss-cross patterns as they rushed to their next class. This is more like it, she thought, as she looked out at the mass of students. The campus looked just as it did when she had been there. Joan shivered with excitement to see so many people going in so many different directions. She confidently stepped off the museum stairs and into the throng, leaving Pablo behind holding his umbrella.

"You're flattering me, Pablo.
My breasts are nothing like these at all....

CHAPTER XIX

argaret paused at the mailbox before going into the house. She was home an hour earlier than usual and and was hoping, to get to the mail before Helen did, just for once. Helen always went through it recklessly, throwing out important things like insurance policies and driver's license renewal notices. Margaret was usually able to retrieve most of it from the recycling bins but that made Helen angry. 'Why do you insist on going through the garbage after I've thrown the mail out? It's just junk,' she would complain.

But the mail hadn't come yet. Instead, there was a large off-white envelope with her name on it in Joan's familiar elegant writing. She put her grocery bags down and opened it quickly, as people usually do with personal mail, in the often vain expectation that something exciting might be inside. But Margaret was disappointed to find not only something that wasn't at all exciting to her but something she had been dreading to receive: ten tickets to the Octoberfest and a nicely written personal note instructing her to sell them all herself. After her initial disappointment, she began to count on her fingers the people she might invite or sell tickets to: Helen, Nel, and Matt, who would all be her guests. Including herself, that was just four. She couldn't see inviting any of her artist friends, except for Matt and Nel, or museum people; they weren't the type for an Octoberfest, and she certainly didn't want to spend any more of her own money. Whoever ended up with the other tickets would just have to buy them.

Then she remembered David next door. He would buy one; too bad he wouldn't bring a friend though: Then he could buy two. She looked over towards his house; everything looked neat and tidy, just as usual. Thank goodness he wasn't sick as Helen had thought in July. Then there were Fred and Elaine; perhaps she could sell them tickets before Joan did. And Annette and Edward, she would have to approach Edward at work, though, since beer and dancing weren't the type of things Annette would go for and she always managed to avoid most of the neighborhood events. Margaret counted again: that made nine, she thought with relief; only one more, and of course it would be Tim. They had had coffee together twice since Nel's dinner party and it had been surprisingly fun. Hadn't he said that he wanted to get to know the people in the neighborhood again? Maybe she would even take the bold step of asking him as a date and pay for the ticket herself. But that might be making a kind of statement about their friendship and she wasn't sure if she wanted to intensify things just yet. She'd have to mull this one over.

As she came down the steps, her eyes fell on an empty hole next to the stairs, and for a few seconds she couldn't remember why it was there or what had been dug up. She stopped and tried to think: either she was loosing her mind, or it hadn't been anything very important, like some building you passed on the way to work everyday that suddenly disappeared and then you couldn't remember what had been there. But then it dawned on her, of course, it was the rhododendron. How could she have forgotten so soon? It was probably these damn tickets, she decided. It was such a relief to think she would be able to get rid of them. If she couldn't sell them, she had already resolved that she would have to buy them out of her own pocket because she didn't have the strength to go against anything Joan wanted.

Joan had always been the strongest member of their family; indeed over the last few years, she had become almost ruthless. Everyone, including friends and acquaintances, did just as Joan told them to do, especially Margaret since she was youngest of the sisters. Helen could sometimes get out of things by being difficult or pretending she didn't understand what was going on, but Margaret, out of habit, always felt she needed to do as she was told. Others, women in the guild for instance, might agree with Joan, in person, to do some specific task and then renege later, but this was rare.

Naturally Joan used beautiful stationery to promote her scheme for selling the Octoberfest tickets. Beautiful Michaelmas daisies bordered the off-white card Margaret dropped as she fumbled for her keys to the house. Picking up the card, her thoughts went back to last year's November guild meeting where Joan was signing people up to sell Christmas cards for the winter fund-raiser. She grimaced as she remembered the uncomfortable silence in the meeting that seemed to go on forever. Poor Colleen; she never stood a chance.

No one ever figured out how Joan knew, how she had fathomed what Colleen was doing. Joan had been at the podium before Colleen came into the meeting and was still there after she left. Of course, Joan must have seen her passing out envelopes to a few select people in the back of the room, but how could she know they were for Colleen's Christmas party? Abruptly, in the middle of the meeting, Joan suddenly announced, "And now Colleen would like to invite us all to her Christmas party on the 23rd at 7:00. I believe it's a buffet dinner, isn't it, Colleen?"

Then there was the silence. Colleen was already standing since she had been sneaking over to the other side of the room to give Karen Olson an invitation, so she was instantly the center of attention. She didn't handle it very well, she started to stammer little spurting noises to the group. Margaret remembered thinking at the time that the next thing she might see would be drool dripping down from the corners of Colleen's mouth. The whole thing was not a pretty sight, but everyone pretended that nothing was wrong and that the entire situation was perfectly natural. All the members had sat very still, with the more polite ones looking down at their notes. Unfortunately for Colleen, the chairs were set up in a circle so most people could glance up at her once or twice. Finally, after what seemed like a very long time, Colleen gave Joan a spiteful look and announced the party so fast that no one could understand her, but it didn't matter since Joan had already told everyone anyway. Margaret had been surprised at how many people actually did go to Colleen's Christmas party after all, it probably had something to do with all the telephone calls Joan had made the week before to encourage people to attend.

Margaret let herself into the house and laid the mail on the desk in the library while still balancing her grocery bag. Then she moved into the kitchen to unload the groceries. Joan would always make you pay. But usually it was by giving out some unpleasant volunteer work that no one wanted to do as a kind of punishment. She had really gotten Colleen good that time and everyone had seen it.

Margaret often felt lucky and a little guilty that she was Joan's sister and therefore exempt from her wrath, or at least her public wrath. Being Joan's sister also offered Margaret some protection from the other guild members, who sometimes gave her more respect than she felt she deserved simply because she was Joan's sister. Everyone was in awe of Joan's ability to organize an event and raise money. Thanks to Pablo coming through with the publicity, the art auction at the museum had done better than ever this year and the Guild members knew it was all due to Joan's ability to promote an event. The year she had chaired the Blanco auction had been their best fund-raising year ever.

Louise was the only person who had dared to cross Joan, but she hadn't started to become assertive with her until after it was obvious to everyone that Joan couldn't stand her no matter what she did; from that point on, Louise had nothing to lose. The other guild members obviously enjoyed it when Joan mimicked Louise or told a funny story about her, since no one liked Louise much. But she was a tireless worker, so Louise had to be tolerated. Even Joan had to admit that. Try as she might though, Louise was no match for Joan. Joan always had the dirt on her, and everyone else for that matter. Joan knew everything first, and used the information to entertain or punish as she saw fit. She had the ability to pounce on people like a duck on a June bug and Margaret had thanked heaven, more than once, that she had never been in Joan's line of fire.

This was why, when Joan decided to make ten specially selected guild members sell ten tickets to people outside of the guild, everyone knew it was a brilliant idea. Back in the den, Margaret opened the drawer of her desk and laid all ten tickets in a safe spot. Like it or not, they would all have to do their part since Joan had put the ball in their court. Each person would be directly responsible to her and no one would dare call up and say they had failed to meet their quota, and thus it was instantly guaranteed that a hundred and ten people would attend the party. The scheme was an inspiration, and resent it as they all might, they had to admit that Joan had just made three thousand dollars for homeless children.

CHAPTER XX

*A*lthough the weather during the first week of September had been hot and unpleasant, by the middle of the second week it had changed to become cool and rainy. Helen, inspired by the change, decided to invite David over for dinner. She was planning on a cozy evening around the fireplace as long as the weather held, but if it warmed up again, she could always open up all the windows and doors to cool off the house. Since he could only come on a Thursday, the day Margaret worked until five, Helen would have to do all the shopping, which she loved, and all of the cooking, which she hated with a passion. It was very disconcerting for her to have to organize a grocery list and make sure that she got everything she needed; it took all the fun out of going to the grocery store.

Thursday morning, at the kitchen table with her coffee cup beside her, Helen spent several hours looking up recipes and making her list. She felt she was making good progress, but then she made the mistake of going to the store before she had had her lunch. Once there, feeling hungry and irritated because of the midday rush, she decided to treat herself to an extra tall, double latté with whole milk instead of her usual nonfat double short. At least it would fill her up until she had lunch.

The store couldn't have been more packed, and by the time she was at the check out line she was feeling very impatient and fed up with trying to find all the things on her list. She had spent most of her time darting back and forth across the crowded store in search of all the things she needed, often in the order they were written on her paper rather than in the order they were placed on the shelves. Normally, her grocery shopping was much more leisurely since she usually didn't have a list.

This business of having a list was very unorganized, she decided, as she visited the dairy case for the third time. And then, as if being hungry and perturbed wasn't enough, she was forced, because the store was so crowded, to use a checker who had been rude to her on several occasions. She determined to watch him closely so she could make sure he didn't scan any items twice, something she was sure he had done once before. She was watching him vigilantly when suddenly she looked down and realized he was scanning an item she hadn't even put into her cart at all.

"I didn't put that in my cart," Helen's voice rang out across the supermarket in an accusing tone. "Nor that either, nor that, nor that, nor that," she yelled, pointing to the rest of the items in the cart.

The man who was checking her groceries stopped passing the items over the scanner and looked through Helen to the woman who was standing in line behind her. "Are these your groceries, ma'am?" he asked the other woman in an obviously irritated tone.

"No," she murmured as she flashed Helen a tentative glance and then quickly moved over to the next line.

Helen, feeling ignored by the checker, turned to the man next to him who was bagging the groceries. As she turned, her elbow upset her coffee cup, which she had placed on the check-writing stand next to the register. Luckily the cup was almost empty and still had its plastic lid, so only a little spilled out as it tumbled onto the checker's table below. Feeling it was best to ignore that little upset since they usually had paper towels to clean things up with anyway, Helen continued her attack.

"Is this some kind of conspiracy on the part of the store to get people to buy things they don't need or want?" she called out to the bagger, a nice-looking man whom she had never seen before.

He smiled a friendly, relaxed smile. "No, ma'am. I'm sure it isn't."

The checker, who was familiar with Helen, took his time in cleaning up the coffee. He took a deep breath as he wiped down the counter and tried to collect himself. "Miss Eastow," he said, having been corrected some time ago that it wasn't Mrs. Eastow or Ms. Eastow, "I believe you pushed this cart up to this cash register." He paused, and Helen was forced to admit that in fact she had. "That is why," he went on slowly, feeling no need to rush since no one was waiting in line behind her, even though the store was quite full and all the other lines were very long, "that is why I assumed these groceries were yours."

"But how could they be mine if I didn't put any of these things into my cart?" she looked over to the bagger for support. It was obvious that she was getting the upper hand.

"Well, Miss Eastow," he said, repeating her name again in a nasty tone, "are you sure that you had a cart?"

"Of course, I had a cart, you silly man. Why would I be standing here with my checkbook out to pay for my groceries if I hadn't gone shopping first?" Helen felt she was being backed up by the bagger, who began to giggle when she said 'silly man,' so she started to laugh too.

"I think we can then presume, Miss Eastow," the checker went on in a haughty manner that made Helen think he was probably a graduate student at the university, "that you have left your cart someplace out in the store and that these are someone else's groceries."

At this suggestion, the wind seemed to go out of Helen's sails. She stopped laughing and began to look around the store. The eyes of all three of them fell at once on an elderly lady who was peering into one cart after another, as if she were searching for something.

"This one must be her cart," the checker said accusingly to Helen. "She looks very upset, thanks to you." He rushed over to where the woman was and began to gently guide her over to his checkout counter.

"I didn't put that in my cart," Helen's voice rang out across the supermarket in an accusing tone. "Nor that either, nor that, nor that, nor that," she yelled.

"Well!" Helen was offended by the checker's rudeness. She looked over to the bagger who smiled. She noticed his name tag; it said 'James'.

"I'm sorry, Miss Eastow. Would you like me to help you find your cart?" She noticed that he had a slight accent.

"That's very kind of you..., James. I'm glad there is still some service in this store. Let's see now, the last thing I remember putting in was bread. I just don't see how this could have happened." She took his arm and steered him towards the bakery. "I finished all my shopping, and then I went to the checkout counter. Look, here's my cart right where I left it, and here's the bread." They both laughed. "I must have put the bread in and then started pushing another cart."

"Well, maybe you looked at something else before you started to leave this area. Or maybe you started talking to someone."

That was it, Helen remembered; she had seen Annette and that aerobics instructor down by the hot dogs. It was because of them that all this nonsense had happened. She glared around the store looking for them. They had obviously run off some place so she turned back to the bagger and smiled. "You're new here, aren't you? Did you get transferred from a different store?"

"Well, yes. How did you know that?"

"Oh, it's common knowledge how you people get transferred around all the time. I don't think it's fair at all," she said as he helped her find another checkout counter. Things had turned out well after all, she decided, but she would still report that checker. He should be fired.

CHAPTER XXI

argaret was surprised when she came home from work that night and found that all the doors and windows of the house were wide open, and that it was freezing inside. It was so quiet at first that she thought Helen had run out for some reason and not closed up the house. But after Margaret closed the back door and several windows, she heard Helen singing in the kitchen in her usual country-western twang.

"Silently the senses abandon their defenses," her voice rang out. How odd to hear a song from *Phantom of the Opera* sung in a whiny nasal voice.

As she stood in the dining room listening to Helen sing, it dawned on Margaret that tonight was the night David was coming over for dinner. Helen would be busy cooking and by this time she would be in over her head with grandiose dinner plans. Margaret quickly figured out that if she reopened all the doors and windows and then sneaked upstairs to her bedroom, she would be able to hide until dinner time. She hurried through the house opening windows as fast as she could, and as she ran, she began to feel almost terrified that Helen might come out of the kitchen at any second to snatch her up and enslave her as a scullery maid. Helen could be so demanding when she felt herself in charge, and the thought of being made to stand at the stove for half an hour stirring some stupid sauce or chopping garlic or onions was repugnant to Margaret.

There would also be the added irritation of having to watch Helen destroy the kitchen while she dirtied every pan and dish in sight. The thought of it all made Margaret move even faster. She was soon upstairs where she grabbed her robe and rushed into the bathroom, quickly locking the door with a sigh of relief. She felt like a kid again with Helen and Joan teasing her and chasing her around the house.

As she soaked in the warm soapy water, she began to envision the dinner party she had once considered having for Tim and Edward. Leaning back in the tub, one foot resting on the hot water nozzle, Margaret imagined what conversations the three of them might have together. But with each conversation she noticed that only she and Tim seemed to be talking while Edward sat silently by consumed with his own problems.

A feeling of irritation and guilt swept over her as she realized that Edward wasn't having any fun at her dinner party and that she needed to placate him. She would have to make him feel better at the expense of the fun conversation she was having with Tim, but what could she say to appease him? She could bring up Matt and the art show for the homeless, but Edward would only complain that a fund-raiser like that was too provincial for an upscale art museum; he would say it was a tradition the museum had outgrown.

Talking about Annette or his clothes would be inappropriate, and they had hashed over old times too much already. Besides, Tim would think they were both unbelievable boors. She watched, as the soap slipped into the water and all the bubbles started to disappear. She just couldn't imagine any subject that would be interesting to Tim and Edward at the same time. Sitting in the tub, she started to feel disillusioned as she thought of Edward and the solemn attitude he'd had all summer. All his little habits, like his obsession for his clothes and his car didn't seem as endearing as they used to, and he had called her twice last week to talk about nothing as far as she could tell.

Suddenly Helen was banging on the door and screaming, "Margaret, I could have used your help, you know!"

"I'll be right out," Margaret answered, feeling secure in her own bathroom with the door locked.

"Never mind, everything's done now," Helen snarled. "I'm going to take a shower. But if you have time, it would help if you brought in some wood."

"Fine." Luckily it didn't matter what she wore in front of David; she'd throw on an old sweatshirt and bring loads of wood into the house. That would appease Helen.

Later in the living room, Margaret turned on the radio and laid the fire. All the doors and windows were still open, and the house was cool enough to warrant lighting the fire even though David wasn't due for another ten minutes.

"I met the nicest man in the grocery store today," Helen said excitedly when Margaret joined her in the kitchen. "His name is James, and he has an accent."

"James?" Margaret repeated. Helen's enthusiasm was a little alarming to Margaret; she couldn't be switching her affections away from David and to another man. It was always a little scary at first, when Helen brought a strange man into the house; usually someone much younger or from a far-off place like California.

There was always an initial period of concern at least until Margaret got to know the person. It was one thing to be in love with the man next door, but to pick up some stranger in the grocery store was something else.

"Do you know his last name?" She cautiously tried to clear an empty space on the counter so that she could slice the bread.

"No, but it will be easy to find out; he works at the store."

"Oh." Margaret was relieved to know where he worked. Her mind jumped ahead to a complete infatuation on Helen's part, and she began to wonder if this time Helen would keep any loyalties to David. Would this new man erase David entirely from Helen's mind as David had erased the bagger who had been transferred to the east side?

It didn't occur to her to wonder what James would feel about Helen because the relationship wouldn't require much contribution on his part. He would simply have to exist, and be available now and then for a conversation in the checkout line and perhaps dinner a few times a year. It was odd to think how little attention she really needed.

The men in Helen's life, like David and Fred, certainly had a lot of respect for her. Some people even seemed to admire Helen for her eccentricities, but she was predictable in an unusual sort of way. You could always count on her to speak her mind, to offer her true opinion; yet she was fiercely loyal and always ready to dislike anyone you disliked, sometimes with a vengeance that could actually be frightening.

Dinner that evening passed along in its usual way. Helen did most of the talking as she entertained Margaret and David with morbid quotations and amusing stories. She told them about her adventures in the grocery store, blaming everything on Annette and Monica and the rude checker that she would have fired tomorrow. Margaret laughed heartily at Annette and Monica's expense, but David became unusually morose, and there was a moment of awkward silence when Margaret couldn't help but wonder if David's lifestyle might be so far removed from someone like Monica's that he disliked her for it.

"That Monica's a bit odd, don't you think? Kind of a flake, I should say. An aerobics instructor; ha!" Helen commented.

"A flake?" David sounded alarmed and his tone surprised Margaret once again.

"Well, all this business with the body, and spending all her time thinking about her looks. Not much upstairs if you know what I mean, the lights are on but nobody's home. The elevator doesn't go to the top floor. You know what I mean, and anyway, isn't the brain a muscle we should exercise just as much as any other muscle? I wouldn't say that hers gets much exercise."

"No, I don't think that the brain is a muscle. The heart is a muscle, but not the brain." Margaret watched a look of panic sweep over David.

But Helen didn't seem to notice and kept up her usual chatter, "Well, it still needs to be used, doesn't it? She'll probably get dementia like that lady in the grocery store today. It just doesn't seem normal to me, all this concern about your body."

Margaret looked at the two of them: David with his sexual preferences and Helen with, well, just being Helen. Then there was herself, a museum curator and unmarried at almost forty. "We're probably the abnormal ones, if anybody is."

"Us?" Helen said, shocked. "What's abnormal about us? Three decent, almost boring people enjoying a dinner together. You probably couldn't find more normal people on the planet," she laughed a mocking laugh, and David nervously joined in. "But that Monica, I don't see what Annette sees in her; she's probably using Annette for something. I wouldn't trust her an inch; what kind of friend would be so wrapped up in her body?"

David stopped eating and put down his fork. "What do you mean you wouldn't trust her?" His voice was demanding in an assertive way that seemed angry to Margaret. Perhaps she was wrong in thinking he had some kind of unfounded resentment for Monica; maybe they were friends after all. It was just like Helen to plunge ahead and offend while being insensitive to some minor hint or even major signal that would be obvious to anyone else.

"I'm sure she's a very good friend—"Margaret started to say, but Helen interrupted her.

"People like her are a dime a dozen. She's probably slept with half the married men in that gym she works at. It wouldn't surprise me if she was blackmailing some of them. How can she afford that little sports car and all those trips she takes to foreign countries?"

"Blackmail?" He put his hand to his head, and Margaret noticed that he had paled dramatically. Even Helen finally saw that he was upset about something. He pushed himself from the table, and both women were immediately at his side, which was quick and easy since he was sitting at the head of the table.

"It's so hot in here," he murmured, as they moved him over to the couch. And of course, it was hot; the house was closed up now, and the fire had been blazing for some time. Luckily he was dressed in the usual Northwest fashion, so they were able to remove several layers of clothing to cool him off.

As Helen fussed over David, Margaret thought how much she must actually care for him. If David were truly sick, it might be good for Helen to have James standing by to help her pick things up, so to speak. But in the meantime Helen's feelings for David seemed unwavering. Looking at the two of them, it was hard to imagine Helen caring for anyone else.

"What you need is a nice piece of fruit tart and a cup of coffee," Helen said as Margaret moved into the kitchen to make coffee and start cleaning up. She felt tired as she stood looking around the room where every pot and pan, the stove, and the counter were all filthy. Well, there was nothing else to do but rinse the dirty dishes and load as many as possible into the dishwasher. Poor David, she thought as she scraped the plates, perhaps he was sick after all.

But then again, he had bought two tickets to the Octoberfest, and he even smiled excitedly as he said 'two.' Who would he bring? She couldn't imagine him showing up with an intimate friend, not out of the blue like that. Wouldn't it be better for him to make a slow process of 'coming out' and announce his gay preference first. Unless he had made some kind of resolution about it all, or a promise to someone he loved. If he did bring a lover to the dance it certainly wouldn't matter to anyone around here. She closed the lid on the dishwasher and locked it. She decided to wait until later to start it. The noise might disturb him.

CHAPTER XXII

On the day of the Octoberfest it was unusually hot, and the Indian summer that had baked everyone at the end September was showing no signs of relief in October. It was still warm at five o'clock when Joan arrived at the community clubhouse to let the oompah band in so they could set up for the evening. The beer would be delivered around six, and guild members would be bringing the food before seven. That left her with nothing to do between five and seven-thirty except to get dressed for the dance. She planned to arrive about seven-thirty or maybe even eight. Too bad she had to go at all, she thought as she parked her car; she wasn't really in the mood to be around a crowd.

Often, during the course of her volunteer work over the last few years, Joan had wondered how she could have let herself become buried in so many volunteer commitments. And lately, she had begun to realize that although she enjoyed organizing social events and fund-raisers, she actually hated going to them. It was a chore to try and talk to people, and the large crowds made her a little nervous, seeming so out of control sometimes. She was tired of trying to motivate people into action and weary of others not doing their jobs. Arriving late and leaving early at a fund-raising event was an acceptable compromise, but sometimes she felt as if she shouldn't have to go at all. Wasn't it enough that she had organized the event? Why did she have to go, too?

As she walked up to the clubhouse, she was surprised to find Tex and a few of the band members already waiting at the door. They were busy talking, and looking over a songbook that Tex was holding in his hand.

"It is very nice to see you here so early," she commented to him as she unlocked the door. "Now, I hope you know your three hours doesn't start until 7:30 and not a minute sooner." She'd have to remember to bring a copy of the contract with her when she came back in case there was any trouble about the agreement they had made.

"I know that, Mrs. Philbrick. I believe in doing a good job in all my business whether it be prunin' or callin'. I just came early so I could get prepared." He sounded kind of sheepish. Maybe she should go a little easier on him, she decided. After all, any act of kindness now would pay off later in his attitude during the event.

"That's fine, just what I would expect from you. You've always done an excellent job and with integrity too, which is the main thing." She watched as he straightened his posture. Obviously integrity was important to him. It was funny how you still found odd pockets of honor and virtue in all sorts of places. He was obviously the type of person who could be trusted. "I was wondering if you would do me a favor? The kegs will be delivered any minute; I'm going to leave the doors open, so all you'll have to do is keep an eye out for them. They'll just come in and set things up; we've used them before. The other guild members will be arriving around seven with the food."

"No problem, Mrs. Philbrick. The place sure does look nice." They both looked around the room admiring the decorations. There was a nice Bavarian-style backdrop against the wall that would be ideal for photos, and the eating area looked like a beer garden, complete with white Christmas lights and artificial flowers. The flowers were a little tacky, but Joan felt that it would add to the fun.

"Thank you. We were here putting the decorations up all day. Well, see you later. I'll be back around eight." She turned and walked over to the doors to begin propping them open.

"Oh, I almost forgot." He ran over to where Joan was standing. His face had such a look of serious concern that, for a second, she thought some snag had come up. "Before you leave, I need to ask you," he said nervously, "is that friend of yours, Louise Marston, going to be here tonight?"

She tried to think why he might be concerned with seeing Louise. Her first thought was that he had done some kind of work for Louise and that she hadn't paid him. It wouldn't be the first time Louise had used some kind of deceitful ruse to get out of paying a decent hard-working person; look at how she treated Terry and Betty. "Does she owe you money?"

"Oh, no, it's nothing like that! I just need to talk to her, about a job I guess you could say."

Joan looked at him and squinted her eyes a bit. It was obvious to her that he was lying, he was clearly nervous. She held her gaze and waited a few seconds to see if he would blurt out something that would give things away, but he didn't. He just stood there looking down at the floor, fidgeting.

"I'm not sure if she's coming or not," she lied. "Do you want me to give her a message?"

"No, thank you, ma'am. I can always call her. That's what I'll do, I'll just call her up. I have her number. Don't you worry about that"." His voice trailed off as he backed away from her.

Now, what could he possibly want with Louise? If he hadn't seemed so nervous, she would have believed it was about a job, but he was obviously lying. She thought it could have something to do with the Octoberfest, but then he would have known if Louise was coming or not; he wouldn't have had to ask her.

She began to wonder if she should, perhaps, go to the event earlier than she planned so that she could keep an eye on Louise and Tex, but the thought of being there before things really got going was repugnant to her. It would be much more fun to arrive after everyone else was there and enjoying themselves. Then she would save herself the anxiety of worrying about the success of the event as she watched people trickle in during the first hour. But if she came too late, she would run the risk of having everyone applaud when she walked into the room, and she wasn't at all sure she'd like that kind of attention. She might have relished it a few years ago, but not anymore.

Turning onto her street, she began to count how many months she had left as guild president. Was it really only halfway over? What was it Denise had said to her when she bailed her out of the mess with the band: 'You need to get off the volunteer treadmill, Joan.' Denise was right about that. This Octoberfest was more trouble than it was worth.

Of course, it had been a great idea and she felt it was something that should have been done by someone, but why always her? She was getting tired of trying to motivate people into doing things like buy a ticket, or go to an auction. Only ten couples had sent their money in from the invitations alone. If it hadn't been for the pre-sale of tickets, she would have been in real trouble. But often people were willing to write out the check, and then felt they had made their donation and didn't need to show up.

She started to count in her head how many people were likely to come and as she counted, she drove past her driveway. Backing up, she pulled in front of the garage but instead of getting out, she stayed in the car and sat staring at her house without focusing on it. Finally, she broke her gaze and looked at the clock. She tried to think what her husband should be doing right now. It was five-thirty: she'd have to get him in the shower if she wanted to take her time getting dressed later. It was irritating for her to think that if she didn't tell him to take a shower, he would never do it. Instead, he'd wait

God knows how long, even until the party was over, to get ready. It was lonely business running everything. Life would be so much easier if there were someone to share the responsibilities with her, or just to talk to about things, like how much could they reasonably ask Fred to work during the school year or what bank branch was the most convenient for them to use? and so on. What she needed was someone to consider things with, like a companion.

She glanced over to the garbage cans lined up on the sidewalk, all three of them full of pine needles. The Doctor had probably spent the whole day sweeping pine needles, which was fine, except that there were plenty of more important things to do. As she pressed the button for the garage door opener, she wished she had someone waiting inside who would sit down and have a drink with her, discuss the day's events; not someone she would have to put into the shower.

The need for companionship, not leadership, was why she continued to try to force the Doctor to make small unimportant decisions about their lives. She kept trying to coerce him into discussing things, but it took energy to keep trying. Tired and with a headache, she put the car in gear and pulled inside the garage. She resigned herself to a lonely evening surrounded by people.

CHAPTER XXIII

When William Philbrick heard the garage door open and Joan park her car, he raced down to the kitchen and braced himself at a safe distance from the back door.

"I just can't wear this outfit," he blurted out defiantly as soon as she came into the house from the garage. He stood in the middle of the room holding his lederhosen and wearing only his underwear; his pager was drooping heavily from the rim of his boxers. He had been nervously waiting for her to come home for about an hour, and although he felt he had firmly made up his mind, that he could not possibly wear this silly outfit, he still couldn't muster up the nerve to get dressed in his regular clothes. He knew he would need Joan's approval for that.

"Of course you're wearing them." She sounded firm and casual in an unnerving way. "You've already tried them on; they fit fine."

"The fit is not the problem. Martin Boyd is sick, so I have to cover his call. I can't possibly go into an operating room dressed like this."

"I don't see why you can't. It will give them all something to talk about, and you'll have a gown on anyway. Take a pair of pants if it makes you feel any better."

"But changing clothes would slow me down. And what if I have to talk with the family?"

"I have no idea, and I'm getting a headache. All I know is that you have to wear your costume. I can't have people not in the spirit of things. Just stop whining and go get dressed."

He stood frozen in the middle of the kitchen. He knew he would have to do as Joan said, but he also knew he would die of embarrassment if he went to the hospital dressed in this foolish manner. When he was at the hospital he was a powerful and respected man who made life and death decisions; he wanted to keep that reverent atmosphere intact because, although it may not have been conscious, it would be difficult for him to live with Joan if he couldn't command some respect at the hospital.

He had married her with the idea that she was a capable person who would run his life smoothly and leave him to his work, but he had no idea just how smoothly or how thoroughly she would arrange things. He watched as she pulled a bottle of wine out of the refrigerator and aggressively began to uncork it. His hand went to his forehead to wipe the sweat off his brow. 'Oh no,' he thought, if he didn't calm down he'd have to take another shower, and he was so proud that he'd remembered to take one before she'd asked him.

Thinking back, he tried to remember if she had started out bossing him around and controlling every aspect of their lives or if he himself had created this monster of control, which was what she had been claiming. He did know that in their first few years of marriage he had resisted her bossiness, but now she maintained that he had manipulated her into this assertive role and that she resented it. Lately she professed that she didn't want to be responsible for making all the decisions in their lives, and that she was tired of it. Well, if she was tired of it then he should be able to dress the way he liked. He started to throw the lederhosen on the floor in protest but hesitated. Joan was struggling with the corkscrew, and the cork was being ground into small pieces. She was getting furious.

On the other hand, maybe he should leave things as they were. Perhaps it would be better not to stir everything up right now. He knew that whenever he got into the car to drive to their favorite restaurant, his first words were always, "Which way do you want me to go?" and he wanted her to tell him. The truth of the matter was that he enjoyed being free from all these mundane decisions, who wouldn't?

He watched as she finally dug the last piece of cork from the bottle and decided that it wasn't a good time to start any conversations which might lead to his inability to make a decision. He might have to go back to therapy with her, 'so you can take some responsibility for your own personal life,' as she had put it, and he didn't want to go through that again. It was bad enough the first time even though they had given up after only a few months.

Neither the therapist, a Dr. Henry Bachiler, nor
William could figure out just what it was that Joan
really wanted or for that matter what she was even
talking about. William did have a suspicion,
though, that just when she had him so well trained,
she was pulling the rug out from underneath him
by wanting him to make more decisions on his
own. This suspicion, because it was just a suspicion
and not rational reasoning, had caused him to feel
confused and bewildered. He didn't know what she
needed from him, and he became even more baffled
when she said that what she wanted was for him to
have the aptitude to figure out what she wanted.
But the fact was, he decided, that she hadn't
consciously comprehended any of this any more
than he had. Besides, aptitude is not a learned
behavior, it's a natural ability which means that it
would be impossible for him to change his ways.

Watching her drink her wine and calm down,
he began to get up enough nerve to become angry
again. Now she was even disregarding what was
best for the hospital. In the past she had supported
his work unconditionally, often times even knowing
what should be done at the hospital before he
knew it himself, like in the early days of the AIDS
epidemic when so many people were in a panic.
Joan had always held a steady course and had
given him infallible advice.

Lately, however, her support and willingness to
sacrifice seemed to be waning, and this business of
his going into an O.R. with a costume on was
definitely out of character for her. He felt disgruntled
as he stood in the kitchen in his underwear. The
idea that she wasn't standing firm, as she usually

did regarding his work, gave him a sense of dread; once Joan got onto a new trend she usually stuck to it with a vengeance. How could he depend on her to rule if she wasn't supportive of him? But, on the other hand, he didn't know how to take away her power, even if he wanted to.

It flashed through his mind that he could accuse her of saying that she wanted him to take on more responsibilities, but then when he tried, she always thwarted him. But he didn't say anything because he knew enough of himself to realize that he didn't want to be bogged down with all these petty things anyway, at least not on a regular basis. Joan was so much better at dealing with these trifles. Naturally, he had never thought any of this out rationally, but he knew in a sense that if he was able to avoid something like deciding on what brand of water heater to buy, he should try and keep it that way. And wasn't this business of running their lives very time consuming? Things like deciding how much of Fred's school to pay for, what rug to have in the living room, or where to bank were very tiresome. Who wanted to think about all these decisions? He certainly didn't.

As the Doctor stood in the kitchen watching her pour another glass of wine, his silent, vibrating beeper suddenly went off taking him so by surprise that he jumped, and since he was wearing only his socks, he slipped and fell onto the floor.

"What is wrong with you?" Joan demanded, without sympathy, as he reached to turn off the pager. "I can't believe you're still not used to that thing; you've had it for a year." She took a sip of wine and stepped over him. "I'm going into the living room to lie down; you need to get into the shower."

Standing up, he decided not to tell her that he'd already taken a shower. Why bother? Instead, he moved to the phone to call the hospital. Maybe he would get lucky and have to spend the evening in the operating room.

CHAPTER XXIV

y the time Joan and Bill arrived at the party it was eight-thirty. As soon as she walked into the room her heart sank. The band was playing and Tex was dancing a square dance all alone in the middle of the room, but no one else was dancing at all, and although it was a good crowd, there was no life in the room. Joan realized that she needed to do something quickly or the party would be a complete failure. The only action in the room was Renee running across the dance floor towards her. Several other people, even a few men, were trailing behind her with concerned looks on their faces.

"Oh, Joan, thank god, you're here. I've been trying to call you all evening!"

"Bill was on the phone. He's on call,"

"There isn't any beer," Renee blurted out. "I came in a little after six. The kegs were supposed to be delivered by then, and they weren't here."

"Well, did you call them?"

"Yes, I called them around 6:45. I thought they were just late. There was only some stupid man in the office who said we had canceled the order and that it was too late to reorder now. Everyone else had gone home. I swear to you, Joan, I just confirmed with them last week," she pleaded in a whiny voice.

"Canceled the order! Who'd have done that?"

"I told him it was impossible and that no one had canceled the order, but he insisted. He said that a very nice lady with a sweet voice had called on Thursday and canceled everything."

A small crowd began to gather around them, and she became aware of Louise standing next to her, smiling.

"Joan, what a fun party," Louise was saying. "Such a good idea not to have any alcohol. People drink too much nowadays anyway. And Tex is just the life of the party; he does your pruning, too, doesn't he?" Joan looked up to where Tex was dancing all by himself in the middle of the room. He had changed into lederhosen and was dancing a kind of jig and he had a pathetic smile on his face. She tried to collect her thoughts and the obvious solution came to her immediately; it irritated her that no one else had done it already. As usual, she was the only one who could arrange things. This is exactly what's making me crazy, she decided, having to always be the one who figures everything out for Bill, the guild, and the church.

"Renee, listen," she grabbed Renee by the arm and squeezed. "Calm down. Now, I want you to go get all the people on the committee and send them out to get beer. Tell them to go to all the local grocery stores and get all the beer they can. We can return it if they don't drink it. And tell them to get some ice. We'll fill up some of those garbage cans with it and put the beer in there. Now hurry!" she commanded, and the party came to life as people hurried around the room with the anticipation of doing something worthwhile and constructive; something for the good of all.

Sitting quietly in a corner of the room with Tim, Margaret had seen Joan arrive and watched as everyone fluttered around her. Not having a beer wasn't much of a crisis for her, and it was certainly nothing that Joan couldn't handle. Tim didn't seem to be too concerned about it either so they had decided to settled down and wait on the sidelines until the party got going. Since Margaret had called him about the tickets, things had taken off a bit, and this was actually their third date. Margaret felt youthful and attractive in a Bavarian dress laced up at the bodice that she had rented at a costume store. It was a relief for her to be dictated by the need to dress in a theme. Tim's outfit, a Guatemalan shirt he had gotten on his travels before medical school, was a nice compliment to hers. It might even pass for German; but then again, he really looked more like a hippie and he certainly seemed much younger than his thirty six years. His blond curly hair needed a cut.

"I think I'm going to have to find another place to live soon."

"It must be hard living with a married couple, and the children... I can't imagine living with two teenagers."

He started to laugh. "They are pretty bad; they listen to the most horrible music."

"Rock music?" The words of a song Fred and Susan used to play all the time popped into her head, 'Where else should I be, all apologies,' she remembered.

"No, I like rock. They listen to some awful stuff that's played on the radio. It's like a mix of a little good music from the past with some modern stuff, but it comes out pretty mediocre. Every song starts out sounding familiar, and the singing sounds like people wailing. I'd much rather listen to rock and roll. There are some new bands coming out now that are really good. I like rap music, too"

Margaret was surprised. This was a side of him she wasn't aware of. Rap music was such a modern thing: the undergraduates in the collections room of the museum always listened to it. Of course, he was a friend of Matt's and she was well aware that artists of all ages seemed to be up on everything that was current, but she had always thought of Tim as being stuck in a lab or a hospital all these years. She had assumed he was like the other doctors she knew, most of whom were uncomfortable socially and unaware of anything modern. Bill was like that, always leaving everything to Joan and very boring to talk to.

Margaret gazed into Tim's eyes and tried to listen with a sympathetic ear, but instead she began to wonder what he would expect from the woman he'd eventually marry. She thought of Joan and how she had changed since marrying Bill. Joan had always been the dominant one of the three sisters, but she had never been so demanding before she got married. Joan had filled in a kind of gap left by Bill. What does Tim want? What kind of gap does he have?

"But it's not the kids," he went on. "It's Annette. She's becoming unbearable."

"Well, she'll be going to Spain next month, so you'll get a break from her then. Maybe she'll come back all relaxed and happy."

"She's not going to Spain. I wish she was, but she canceled her trip." He sounded disheartened. "I was thinking for a while that she was getting too much exercise, she's so thin, you know, but she's not jogging as much as she used to. Now she's more irritable than ever, and she can be so cruel to Edward. Sometimes I think she only cares about herself. Edward's pretty selfish like that too, worrying about his clothes all the time, but you still get the feeling he cares about his family. Maybe she should go back to taking her evening jogs."

"But you don't think their marriage is in trouble?" Margaret heard herself blurting out. The thought of their getting divorced and Edward running to her for comfort suddenly loomed before her. Her feelings for him hadn't changed too much. There was still a little silent devotion and some love from a distance, but she wasn't ready to take over for Annette. That wouldn't be pleasant at all. And besides, lately he had become very boring and self-centered; or more to the point, lately I realized how self-centered he always was, she decided.

"It wouldn't surprise me in the least if their marriage was in trouble. In fact, I don't see how they can go on with all this tension in the air. It could be that it's always been like this with them, but I don't think so."

As Margaret paused to think things over, she looked to the other side of the room and noticed Annette and Edward walking over the dance floor towards them. Not dressed in costume, they looked out of place among the other party-goers, and both seemed angry as they made their way across the room. Margaret felt for a minute as if she and Tim had been sneaking out on a date and that his parents had come to take him home. It wasn't until Annette and Edward were standing over them that Margaret realized Tim's hand was resting on hers. She jerked it away quickly, almost as a reflex.

"Joan saved the day," Edward said without enthusiasm as he waved a beer in his hand.

"Oh, good. I'll get us a couple." Tim left and walked over to where the beer was.

After what Tim had told her it seemed obvious to Margaret that Edward and Annette had just had an argument. As the three of them sat around the table in awkward silence she could feel the tension between them growing, and she was beginning to think she was in some kind of family scene. But before she could come up with an innocuous remark, Annette suddenly rushed off. Margaret thought that Edward would probably go after her but he didn't seem to notice, even though Margaret had to quickly reach out to keep Annette's chair from crashing to the floor.

Left with Edward she wondered if she should try to say something kind and reassuring to him. But what? She felt sorry for him, but it seemed so self-righteous to pity him. She looked at him more closely: he was slumped over his beer in an uncharacteristic way, and he seemed so disheartened. But this could be just another attempt on his part to have every one focus on his problems, and Margaret couldn't get from her mind the image of his divorcing Annette and running to her. She had never hoped for that scenario to unfold, and a kind word at the wrong moment just might encourage things. Still it was hard not to offer him some kind of comfort, however cold.

"You don't seem to be much in the spirit of things," she finally said, referring to his clothes, a perfectly tailored charcoal wool suit.

At this he seemed to perk up a bit and even managed a smile. "No, I didn't have a costume that would look right, and I couldn't see myself throwing something together."

But Margaret didn't hear what he was saying; instead she was watching Helen standing on the edge of the dance floor talking with David and a very attractive blond. David had his arm around the woman and was pulling her close to him in an affectionate way. He looked happy and relaxed. Helen's back was to Margaret, but she could see that David and the other woman were laughing. So that was who he had bought the other ticket for; she thought back to how excited David had been when he gave her the money.

For the second time in the past few months, Margaret found herself trying to sort through her misconceptions of another person's sexuality, first Susan and now David. She had obviously been wrong about both of them. She wondered why she had assumed all this time that David was gay, but try as she might, the only answer she could come up with was that Helen had told her so. Margaret felt ashamed of herself for believing Helen since she had learned over the years not to trust anything she said, especially when it involved Helen's opinion of things. But in her obsession with him, Helen had almost owned David as far as Margaret was concerned. They were much better 'friends', if you could call it that, than Margaret and he were. Margaret had just assumed Helen knew what she was talking about where David was concerned. But actually, Margaret remembered suddenly, that about a year and a half ago she had seen a very attractive woman leaving David's house after dark in a black Surburban. She had, at the time, dismissed what looked like a good-bye kiss at the door and had not thought about it since.

Poor Helen, Margaret thought, as she watched them all laughing. This would be a lot worse than when Helen had spent the whole summer pining for the grocery clerk who was transferred to another store. She had even driven across the lake to the eastside to do her grocery shopping, just so she could see him. But then David had moved in next door, and Helen had found a new interest. Margaret glanced back at Edward. He seemed content just sitting there in silence, which was fine with her. It was more fun to focus on the crowd anyway. She looked around the room once again and this time she caught sight of Annette.

Storming across the dance floor, in an effort to catch up with her brother, Annette caught sight of David and his date. How dare he? she thought, when he had vaguely broken things off with her less than a month ago, bring a date to a party where he knew she'd be! Well, there was nothing left for her to do but to grab her husband and go home immediately with a smile on her face, she decided as she paused for a second in the middle of the room. She certainly wasn't going to let David see her leaving alone and upset. But first she wanted to have a talk with her little brother, and the sight of David and another woman, an attractive blond, made her more determined than ever to set Tim straight.

When she finally caught up with Tim she jerked at his sleeve to stop him. "I don't get this, are you going out with Margaret? Tell me this isn't so?"

"Annette, what is with you? She's one of your oldest friends. Something is wrong with you lately. I don't know what it is, but leave me out of it. It's none of your business who I go out with, anyway. Why do you always think that everything I do is your business?" He jerked his arm away from her and wiped off his sleeve.

"She's at least five years older than you. Could you see her having kids at her age?"

"She's only three years older than me, Annette, and like I said, don't worry about it! Why don't you try and straighten out your own life instead of worrying about mine so much?"

He left Annette standing alone in the middle of the room where she crossed her arms in front of her and looked disdainfully around at the party. Some silly man dressed in lederhosen was leading a small group of people on the dance floor while the band played an absurd German folk tune that was so loud she could feel the floor vibrate. The sight of Margaret and Edward sitting awkwardly in the corner nauseated her. What was she going to do now? She certainly wasn't going to stay around here. It was an easy walk home, and it would serve them right if she just disappeared. They could spend the whole evening looking for her for all she cared. But then she looked back over towards David. Luckily his back was turned to her so he hadn't seen her lose control. She needed to leave as soon as possible.

She stormed back to the table where Margaret and Edward sat. "I've had enough of this, we're leaving!" She grabbed Edward's arm possessively.

"What's wrong?" He stood up, surprised yet ready to obey her.

Margaret started to say good-bye but she felt paralyzed. Annette hadn't acknowledged her and now she was giving her a scathing look that clearly said, *How dare you try to steal my husband?*

Was this the problem between them? Margaret wondered as feelings of embarrassment and shame overwhelmed her. She felt like a wounded deer locked in the headlights of Annette's eyes. Had Annette figured out everything after all these years? Suddenly she felt so foolish. Annette's words, 'I've had enough of this,' rang in her ears. What an idiot she had been to think that Annette would never find out about her and Edward. The last few months quickly flashed through her mind: Edward and his change of attitude towards her after she had disagreed with him at the May board meeting, and his wanting to come to dinner when Annette was in Spain... even inviting himself in front of Annette. And then Tim moved back to town and he wanted to spend time with her too; she looked up to see him walking towards her with two beers in his hands, a worried look on his face. And tonight Edward had seen Tim holding her hand. Had he said something about it to Annette as the two of them walked over to the table? It would be just like Edward to make some jealous remark about her and Tim without realizing that he was talking to his wife. But before she could think it all through, Edward and Annette had left and Tim was standing over her.

"Don't let Annette get to you," he said, handing her a beer. So Annette had told him about her and Edward. Embarrassment flooded over her. She hadn't felt so foolish in years.

"What do you mean?" She nervously took a sip of her beer.

"I just mean, don't buy anything she says; she's been a pain in the neck for as long as I can remember. She's always wanted to control my life and ever since we were kids she's thought she had the right to pick and chose who I go out with. I think what she really needs to do is to figure out her own problems. They need to do something about their marriage. I don't know what the problem is, but you know what, I don't think I even care."

Margaret sat back in the metal folding chair and listened with a growing sense of relief as he talked. Annette obviously hadn't said anything about her and Edward. Maybe she didn't even know about them. Maybe it was the idea of Tim and herself that made Annette so angry. She was aware of a calming sensation coming from her beer and she drank it down faster than she normally would have.

Out on the dance floor the party started to take off as people celebrated the arrival of the beer with marked enthusiasm. A whole hour without alcohol had taken its toll on the crowd, and now it was as if some kind of prohibition had been lifted. Even the band, which had taken a break when the beer arrived, became more exuberant. Joan was standing on the sidelines watching when the band started up again. Everyone rushed out to the dance floor immediately, many with beers in their hands. Most of the crowd was in costume, and it seemed to spur on the feelings of wild abandonment in the room. Joan smiled in wonderment; she had never seen so many people having so much fun. They seemed absolutely desperate to have a good time.

She calculated that she had actually made an extra three hundred dollars because the beer had been cancelled. During the 'crisis' it seemed as if almost everyone had given her money, mostly twenty-dollar bills, to cover the emergency. Everything had worked out fine, she decided as she watched Margaret and Tim begin a polka dance. On the other side of the room she could see Helen in a line dance that Tex was leading; Fred and Susan were lined up behind her. Too bad Bill was called to the hospital just as things got going, she thought. He could stand to loosen up a little.

The only people not dancing were two women over in a dark corner of the hall by the bathroom doors. Curious to see who they were, Joan moved closer to where they were standing. They looked to her as if they were angry about something, but not at each other, since they were whispering back and forth in each other's ears. Then Joan was able to make out their faces; they were Louise and Colleen. Suddenly the words 'a very sweet lady' rang in her ears.

"Joan, my darling, we never had that lunch," a voice hissed at her, interrupting her thoughts. "I saw your husband leaving the dance, so you're all alone, aren't you?"

Joan turned in surprise. "Why did he always have to stand so close?" she wondered as she inhaled Pablo's breath; he smelled like Scotch, the irritating little man. Of course he wasn't dressed in costume, and he had started to grow a beard, to go with his ponytail, no doubt.

"I took care of all your needs, and you took care of none of mine. I think that you used me, Joan, and I don't care much for that," he accused her as he looked around the room. "You could have at least had your maid call me."

"My maid?" Not only was she appalled by his audacity but she was confused by what he'd said. She looked out onto the dance floor where several middle-aged women in pigtails were dancing. "Milkmaids?" she wondered vaguely.

"Are you talking about my cleaning ladies?"

"Yes, of course. They aren't here tonight by any chance, are they? I would forgive you if they were, you know." He actually leaned forward and pushed a strand of hair off her face.

"Why, yes, one of them is here..." she answered, excited by her own brilliance. It was odd to think how the best ideas just popped into one's head. Creativity all happened on the subconscious level, she mused as she added, "...over there by the bathroom, the one on the left. Her name is Louise."

"Aha! Where?" He brightened up. "There? The one in that short square-dancing outfit?"

"Yes, that's the one. Ask her to dance. You know, Pablo, she'll never work for you unless she likes you; there's such a demand for truly good house-cleaners. They can really pick and choose whom they work for." Which was actually true. "So don't mention the cleaning business until she's gotten to know you. Be persistent though; don't give up." He certainly knows how to do that, she thought. "She used to work as an erotic dancer," she went on, feeling as if she had reached a creative pinnacle, "so she's used to giving men the brush-off. It's second nature to her. But she still loves to dance..." her voice trailed off since he was already halfway across the room.

CHAPTER XXV

ere, try this on your eye." Louise offered an uncooked hamburger patty to her husband for the third time that morning. Except for a couple of groans, he had yet to answer her.

"Louise, will you leave me alone?" Brian finally snapped. "I'm not going to put raw hamburger on an open wound. I could get an infection. I might even get E. coli poisoning for all I know!"

"But it's supposed to be good for black eyes," she insisted as she fussed with his ice pack. She'd had about enough of this irritable mood of his.

"You're supposed to use steak for a black eye, not hamburger."

"Well, what's the difference?" That was it. She'd reached the limit of her patience. After all, she had been catering to him all morning. It wasn't like him to be so hateful towards her, and he wasn't going to start now. Last night, as bad as it was, was no excuse for his acting like this all day. Fine! she decided, as she stormed out of the room. She would just leave him with his misery.

Later, out on her deck with a heavy coat over her shoulders, Louise tried to piece together just what had happened last night. It seemed like such a long evening now that she had a chance to think back on it. She smiled as she thought of Pablo, that handsome friend of Joan's, asking her to dance. How good-looking and chic he was with his ponytail and scruffy beard. And it was so obvious, from the very first, that he was really taken with her. Why, he seemed absolutely in love with her. 'I need you desperately,' he had whispered in her ear in a breathy low voice that still gave her the tingles when she thought about it.

But then the music had stopped, and suddenly Brian was pulling them apart and screaming at her. "Louise, did you tell this man you wanted him to help you have twins?"

She looked at Pablo. No, she hadn't told him that. She hadn't even thought about it, not exactly at least. But before she could answer, Tex was there.

"Louise, I'm so sorry, but I thought he knew about it. You said he knew all about us the last time I saw you." By this time the room was quiet, the band had stopped playing and a crowd was gathering around them. All she had wanted to do was go on dancing with Pablo. As her eyes rested on the opposite shoreline of the lake, she wondered, not for the first time that day, if she would ever see Pablo again. He had disappeared mysteriously when Brian started screaming. He must have felt guilty about his feelings towards her, she decided. Brian had obviously scared him off. But she couldn't figure out why Tex had gotten involved. And after Tex came up to them, what had happened then? All she could remember was that Brian had slugged Tex, who was twice his size, and then a band member had hit Brian. After that it was all a blur, the party turning into a brawl between the band members, who were young and strong, and the neighborhood men, who were middle-aged and out of shape.

But the bottom line of what really had happened, she resolved, was that three men, if you counted Pablo, had literally fought over her at a party. 'Should I be embarrassed?' she wondered vaguely as she watched some water fowl circling the lake. She certainly didn't need to be ashamed of anything she had done with Pablo, all she did was dance with him; and for her husband to care so deeply for her that he gotten into a fight, well, not many women, after fifteen years of marriage, could boast of that kind of love. She tried to imagine, for a brief second, Brian loving her with that kind of passion. It was hard to fathom where had it suddenly come from. Could it be that these romantic feelings had been smoldering away in him all this time? It didn't seem likely. But she quickly dismissed any doubts she may have had concerning Brian's passion. After all, she had seen him with her own eyes: he had punched Tex in the nose, there was no doubt about it.

Then her thoughts turned to Tex, and she began to laugh when she remembered what Brian had said to her. Me have a baby, twins! With Tex, a tree pruner! And what was all this business about fertility problems? How absurd that was. All Brian would do was shake his head when she had asked him about it last night coming home in the car. But then this morning he had muttered, under his breath, some little snide remark about how she would do anything to get rid of Joan's tree and the whole thing had poured out. Of course she was able to quickly straighten things out with Brian because number one, nothing had been cut off the tree; and number two, what did any of this have to do with her having Tex's baby or anyone's baby for that matter. Tex's accusation about her having his baby was too outrageous to be taken seriously by Brian or anyone else. Her reputation could remain intact because she had done nothing to provoke any of this nonsense. How was it her fault if men still found her attractive?

It was exciting to think that Brian had rushed to defend her honor, to fight for her love, so to speak; even if he had punched the wrong man, she thought giggling. But, perhaps it would be a new beginning for their marriage, the start of a new passion between them. Of course this morning was no indication of a new beginning of any kind, but then again Brian probably just needed a little time to recover from his head injuries.

"And to think that I managed to ruin Joan's party after all," she thought, delighted with herself. "Seven more months and I'll be guild president," she sang out loud. "And then I can boss Joan around all I want."

CHAPTER XXVI

$\mathcal{F}$n the coffee line at the bakery, Margaret
noticed the girl in front of her. 'This must
be the retro look,' she thought to herself,
'heavy black laced-up boots and scrunched-up
socks over leggings. No, that wasn't the retro look,
or was it? Shouldn't there be some body piercing
and platform shoes instead of boots?' She'd have to
remember to ask someone at the museum about it.

"Have you heard from Angela lately?" the
cashier was asking the girl in the boots.

"No, I haven't heard from her. She's in Italy.
Courtney told me she's in love."

Margaret's thoughts drifted to Rome, the
Spanish Steps and love. What was Angela doing
right at this moment? Possibly she was sitting in
some streetside cafe sipping cheap wine with her
beautiful Italian lover, discussing art with a
group of students or perhaps she was just waking
up. Margaret glanced at her watch and began

calculating the time difference. It was probably night-time in Rome right now.

"A single short latté?" the cashier queried, jolting Margaret back to reality. She looked up to see several people staring at her. It was nice that the cashier remembered her usual order, but suddenly she felt like something stronger.

"A double cappuccino," she blurted out.

"A double cappuccino," the girl called in a clear voice to the clean-cut young man working the machine.

At a table in the corner, Margaret sat down and began organizing her afternoon. On her way out of the house she had picked up the mail so she could look through it while she drank her coffee, but she wasn't sure what to do about recycling all the junk mail. She hated to just throw it into the garbage at the Village.

'Of course I could always carry it back home,' she thought wearily.

Feeling slightly overwhelmed by the trivialities of daily life, she decided to go over her grocery list before she looked at the mail. That would take only a second since she had already worked on it at home. She just needed to add cranberries for the relish she was making to take to Joan's for Thanksgiving. She fished through her coat pocket looking for the list, but she couldn't seem to find it. She pulled out several receipts and notes to herself and after both of her pockets were empty, she finally noticed that the list was on the first paper she had pulled from her pocket. It hadn't looked like her grocery list because Helen had written a quotation on the other side.

'I hear a voice you cannot hear, which says I must not stay; I see a hand you cannot see, which beckons me away.' She read it once more. The words sounded familiar, it was probably from a poem she had read in poetry class during college. Although it was a beautiful quotation that rang true, she quickly decided it would never do for their mother's grave. It reminded her more of two lovers parting or of someone at a crossroads than of a spirit moving up to heaven. It had too much of a physical quality, that was it, she thought; even though it was profound, it lacked spiritualness in the literal sense. She turned the paper over and made her note about the relish on the other side and then started going through the mail.

Not much there, the whole bunch of it was junk mail, definitely too much to just throw away. She would feel guilty all day if she wasted perfectly good recyclable paper in the garbage; she would just have to carry the whole pile back home. She had started to tie it all back up with a rubber band when she noticed a letter that had been stuffed into a grocery store coupon flier. It had the guild's letterhead and was in Joan's handwriting. Not very exciting, she thought, but at least it would be something to read.

Dear Guild Members:

Thank you for allowing me to be your guild president. I have truly enjoyed working with all of you. Due, however, to my increased family commitments and my new hobby, gardening, I feel you would all be better served by another president. I have also decided to resign from the guild so that I can pursue my new hobby.

At this time, I would like to invite all of you to join me as charter members of the Lakeview Garden Club. Our first meeting will be at 10:00 a.m. on January 15 at my home, where Tex, from Tex's Tree Service will talk about "Trees in the Northwest." Tex will also demonstrate how to plant a tree in my front yard, where he will be planting a companion to my deodara.

Best wishes for a wonderful holiday season!

Fondly,
Joan Philbrick

Joan had warned her that she was thinking about resigning from the guild, but she had not mentioned anything about a gardening club. 'What a good idea,' Margaret thought as she sipped her coffee. Perhaps they could get someone in to lecture on the care of rhododendrons. She'd have to make sure Helen was there for that one.

"I see you're on your sister's mailing list," a familiar voice that sounded both accusing and angry caught her by surprise.

"Oh, hello, Louise." Margaret tried to sound casual but Louise's appearance was startling. Her hair was completely disheveled and she seemed very upset. "Have a seat," Margaret offered, but Louise kept standing.

"Sweet, isn't it?" Louise finally said, motioning towards the letter that was laying open on the table.

"Sweet? Well yes…" Margaret tried to think what could be sweet about Joan's letter. "I guess you'll have to take over the guild sooner than you expected."

She tried to sound bright and cheerful, but she couldn't think of what Louise meant by 'sweet.' Maybe that Louise would finally get to be guild president, but it seemed like an odd choice of words. "And a garden club, everyone will love that."

"Humph! I think this is just another one of Joan's stunts."

"Well, Louise, don't take it like that. You don't have to be president until next year if you don't want to. I'm sure something could be worked out." Louise seemed to take little consolation in what Margaret was saying. She plopped down in a chair and sighed a sigh of exhaustion.

"But it would hardly be any fun without Joan there to boss around."

Margaret smiled. She was touched and surprised to think that Louise could be so downtrodden at the thought of Joan leaving the guild. Why, she looked almost as if she were about to cry, or even depressed if you considered her appearance.

"And the tree, I can't believe she's planting another tree with that idiot Tex," Louise went on, almost to herself.

"Well, don't worry about that. You can skip the first meeting and still be a charter member; you don't have to see Tex. And, anyway, everybody will have forgotten about the Octoberfest by then."

Margaret drained the last drop of coffee from her cup. She thought back to the Octoberfest and tried to sort through the facts as she could remember them. It was all very confusing since there were a lot of crazy rumors still going around and every story was so different that she had never figured out what really happened. She was sure, though, that contrary to what people were saying, Louise was not having an affair with either Pablo or Tex. One seemed as farfetched to be linked with Louise as the other.

Margaret looked at her again, she was all slumped over and unkempt, not at all like her usual self. This would probably be a good time to drag the whole story out of her since she looked so crushed and almost vulnerable, but it didn't seem right to take advantage of her misery, especially when she was down about Joan leaving the Guild. And Joan would find out everything about the Octoberfest sooner or later anyway. That kind of thing was more up her alley.

Margaret leaned over to where the garbage was and threw her cup away, then she stood up to leave. She didn't like to leave Louise in such a state but then again, she was probably meeting someone for coffee. "If I don't see you, have a nice Thanksgiving."

"You, too." Louise mumbled the words so weakly that Margaret could barely hear her. She felt a little guilty walking out on her, but she had tried to cheer her up. People so often became depressed over the holidays, and poor Louise didn't seem to have many close friends. Maybe some of the rumors going around about her were true after all. She did seem almost desperate.

CHAPTER XXVII

*T*ap, tap, tap. Fred stood up from the table and began tapping his glass. Margaret knew what he was about to announce, and she was excited and ready to hear.

"First, I want to say Happy Thanksgiving to everyone." He raised his glass and paused as he looked around the table. "Especially to our guests today, David, Heather, and Tim. It was so nice of Annette and Edward to go on a second honeymoon and leave you with us for the holiday, Tim."

"And especially nice of Edward's parents to invite the kids over for the day." Tim wiped his brow in comic relief as everyone laughed. Margaret worried, once again, that it was unhealthy for him to still be living with Annette and Edward. Things had gotten a little better since Edward and Annette had started going to a marriage counselor, but it was still stressful for him. He needed to move out as soon as possible. He should rent that apartment they had looked at last Sunday; it was perfect for one person. "What was he waiting for?" she wondered as she lifted her glass in a toast to him. He was smiling from ear to ear. Everyone else lifted their glasses to him too and took a sip of wine. Then they all turned to Margaret and did the same to her, as if they were joining them together in the same toast. Margaret felt comfortable and relaxed surrounded by her family and friends at the end of a wonderful Thanksgiving dinner, and especially happy with Tim across the table from her. She turned to acknowledge everyone's toast, bowed her head a little, and then giggled.

"Here's to Margaret." Tim raised his glass again to her and everyone followed. But, although Margaret was enjoying all the attention and kindness from her family, it was Fred and Elaine's moment. She took a sip of wine and turned back to Fred.

But he was smiling at her too, in no hurry to move the focus to himself. "Here's to Aunt Margaret."

"Okay, enough already." Margaret laughed. "Didn't you have something to say, Fred? You shouldn't be playing around at the dinner table, you know. We taught you that years ago."

"What? An announcement?" Fred was trying to tease them all, but it wasn't working very well. Everyone knew what he was going to say. "Oh, yeah. No, seriously everyone," he went over to Elaine and put his arms around her. She raised her hand and let it rest on his arm. "We would like to invite you all to a wedding on the 26th of December. Elaine and I are going to be married."

Everyone let out a cheer and tapped their glasses together in a toast to the two of them. As she looked back to Fred with admiration, an article she had read recently about Thanksgiving flashed through her mind: *Raising Kids, It All Boils Down to Thanksgiving Dinner.* She had thought about him a lot as she read it, especially about how well he had turned out.

It was true, really, you should simply raise your kids to be someone you would want to have Thanksgiving dinner with for the rest of your life. Good table manners, of course Fred had those. Not be a racist, that was easy since no one in their family was like that. A person should be educated so they can make good dinner conversation... everyone had helped with that one; Bill had done his part with math and science and Margaret had helped teach Fred about history in the back-room of the museum. Also, a person shouldn't drink too much and ruin everyone's meal or sneak off to smoke marijuana between courses. And, of course, one should be kindhearted and thankful; Fred was certainly that.

Helen, lifting up a pie to show everyone, was absolutely gushing with good cheer and best wishes. "Now, it's congratulations to the groom and best wishes to the bride," she was reminding everyone as she began cutting into a pecan pie. James, the bagger at the grocery store, had recommended the gourmet pecans to her especially. "Now, everyone has to have some of James's pie"

Looking over to Joan and Bill, Margaret noticed how relieved they looked. She watched as they turned to each other and toasted themselves in a private, almost romantic way. Perhaps, finally having an empty nest would help Joan relax.

And David and his date Heather from the Octoberfest were enjoying a private moment also as they gazed into each other's eyes. Margaret felt Tim's eyes on her and looked over to him. He was staring at her, but not with a big grin this time; now he had only a half smile with a look of quiet devotion and affection. She leaned back into her chair and smiled; there was really so much to be thankful for this year.

CHAPTER XXVIII

*B*ride or groom?" Margaret heard the handsome young man in the tuxedo ask the two young girls in line in front of her. They had both removed their wet raincoats and looked more like they were going to a prom than a wedding in their short, spiffy dresses. But of course, they would probably look more in place at the reception, she decided.

"Bride," one of them answered.

"Bride?" the usher asked in a flirtatious way. "You know the bride?" He sounded surprised even though nothing could have been more natural than the notion that they were friends of the bride.

"We went to high school together," one of them said as she flipped her hair from one side to the other.

"And college," chimed in the other one. "We were roommates in college."

"Then why aren't you in the wedding party?" he teased.

"Because, she has three sisters," the hair-flipper answered, laughing.

"I see. Well, in that case I'll have to seat you right up front in a place of honor. Ladies?" he said as he put out both of his arms, much as someone would do if he were pretending to be a chicken flapping its wings. He spun around, and each of the girls took an arm. Margaret watched as the three of them walked slowly up the church aisle. It went through her mind that she need not worry about Elaine running off to New York the way Susan did, not with friends like these.

She felt a little pang of sadness for a moment as she thought of Susan. Margaret hoped she had found happiness in New York with her new life. Elaine suddenly seemed very different from Susan, a bit shallow perhaps? Margaret could never imagine Susan having friends like that, and yet perhaps they were more Fred's type after all. It was probably a good sign, she decided.

"Bride or groom?" a different young man in a tuxedo asked her. But before she could answer, he blurted out, "You're Margaret Eastow, Fred's aunt from the museum board."

Margaret was struck by how impressed he seemed to be with her. Was this her fifteen minutes of fame?

"I'm Jay Swaine," he said. For a second Margaret was at a loss, but then remembered he was the artist friend of Fred's who had been having some success at local galleries. "Will Matt Weeks be here?" he asked perking up even more.

"Yes, I'm sure he will be. Our side had a little difficulty coming up with enough people to balance out the bride's. We invited everyone," she added, immediately feeling as if she had said too much. But he didn't seem to have heard her, he was busy straining his neck to peer over her shoulder.

"I'll see him at the reception if I miss him here," he mumbled almost to himself as he put an arm out for her to take.

When they turned to walk down the aisle, Margaret was struck by how beautiful the church looked. She had never been in St. Anne's before and, in fact, she had hardly been to any churches during the evening, except for Christmas Eve services, which her family almost never attended since they were always too busy eating their Christmas duck.

There was a mysterious and romantic feeling about the church with all the candles glowing along the sides of the nave in the darkness. All the rows were posted with arrangements of yellow roses that had gold and white ribbons cascading onto the floor, and the altar was flanked with large sprays of matching flowers.

The holidays and romance together created an unrealistic sensation that seemed to be out of place in a church. But, of course, it was a wedding, she told herself. And what better place than a church to adapt itself to the needs of the people; to the flow of life.

Several people turned to smile at her as she walked down the aisle, and she saw that Matt and Nel were already seated. She felt badly for the young artist who wanted to meet Matt. Oh well, he would have to find him at the reception. Then she passed David and Heather sitting with some other people from the neighborhood. Next, she noticed

Edward and Annette, and she was both surprised and relieved to see that they were holding hands. She felt as if she had made a narrow escape there, and she was happy to see that they had patched things up. As the usher seated her next to Helen, she became aware that Tim had been following her down the aisle.

"Do you mind if I sit with you?" he asked in a whisper after he sat down.

She didn't mind at all, but before she could answer Helen said a little too loudly to both of them, "I've arranged for James to get a job with the caterers. He'll be helping with the espresso machine at the reception, and he'll get fifty dollars! So much better than bagging groceries at the supermarket."

Margaret looked at Tim, and they both raised their eyebrows at the same time and smiled. Then the music started, and the wedding began.

She didn't mind at all

GOODFELLOW PRESS

Novels from Goodfellow Press are smooth and seamless with characters who live beyond the confines of the book covers.

Ivory Tower by May Taylor. Does the scent of lilacs herald a soft haunting?
ISBN 0-9639882-3-9 $12.99/$13.99 Canada.

Cookbook from Hell by Matthew L. Buchman. One part creation. Two parts software. Season lightly with a pair of love stories and roast until done.
ISBN 0-9639882-8-X $12.99/$13.99 Canada

The Inscription by Pam Binder. An immortal warrior has conquered death. Now he must conquer living.
ISBN 0-9639882-7-1 $12.99/$13.99 Canada.

Matutu by Sally Ash. To find healing and love, an English violinist and an American writer must explore a Maori legend.
ISBN 0-9639882-9-8 $12.99/$13.99 Canada.

Bear Dance by Kay Zimmer. A man betrayed and a woman escaping painful memories struggle to overcome the barriers keeping them apart.
ISBN 0-9639882-4-7 $9.99/$10.99 Canada.

White Powder by Mary Sharon Plowman. Itís hard to fall in love when bullets are flying. ISBN 0-9639882-6-3 $9.99/$10.99 Canada.

Glass Ceiling by C.J. Wyckoff. Facing career and emotional upheaval, Jane Walker makes a bold choice to explore East Africa with an unorthodox man. ISBN 0-9639882-2-0 $9.99/$10.99 Canada.

This Time by Mary Sharon Plowman. A man and a woman with differing expectations and lifestyles, take a chance on love.
ISBN 0-9639882-1-2 $7.99/$8.99 Canada.

Hedge of Thorns by Sally Ash. A gentle story unfolding like a modern fairy tale, of painful yesterdays and trust reborn.
ISBN 0-9639882-0-4 $7.99/$8.99 Canada.

Homework:Bridging the Gap by Kay Morison, Ph.D/Suzanne Brady. Empowers parents, teachers and students to solve the homework dilemma.
ISBN 0-9639882-5-5 $12.99/$15.99 Canada.

A Slight Change of Plans by John H. Zobel. Mike Archer has a chance to solve a mystery and meet the girl of his dreams if only he can get out of the moose suit. ISBN 1-891761-01-3 $12.99/$13.99 Canada.

The Songs of Kalaran by Matthew Lieber Buchman. How should you treat your mother when she heads the interstellar mafia and you don't remember her? ISBN 1-891761-C4-8 (Released 1999)

GOODFELLOW PRESS
16625 Redmond Way, Ste M20
Redmond, WA 98052-4499
(425) 881-7699
Available from: Partners Publishers Group

An Unobstructed View

(AS YOU LIKE IT)

16625 Redmond Way, Ste M20
Redmond, WA 98052-4499
(425) 881-7699

1. How would you rate the following features? Please circle:

	Unfavorable			favorable	
Overall opinion of book	1	2	3	4	5
Character development	1	2	3	4	5
Conclusion/Ending	1	2	3	4	5
Plot/Story Line	1	2	3	4	5
Writing Style	1	2	3	4	5
Setting/Location	1	2	3	4	5
Appeal of Front Cover	1	2	3	4	5
Appeal of Back Cover	1	2	3	4	5
Print Size/Design	1	2	3	4	5

2. Approximately how many novels do you buy each month?_____
   How many do you read each month?_____

3. What is your education?
   High School or below _____   College Graduate _____
   Some College   _____   Post Graduate   _____

4. What is your age group?
   Under 25 _____   36-45 _____
   26-35   _____   46-55 _____   Over 55 _____

5. What types of fiction do you usually buy? (check all that apply)
   Historical   _____   Western   _____
   Science Fiction   _____   Action/Adventure   _____
   Romantic Suspense   _____   General Fiction   _____
   Mystery   _____   Time Travel/Paranormal _____

6. Why did you buy this book? (check all that apply)
   Front Cover   _____   Know the author   _____
   Like the characters _____   Back Cover   _____
   Like the ending   _____   Heard of publisher   _____
   Like the setting   _____   Purchased at a book signing_____

For current Goodfellow Press updates:
   Name_____
   Street_____

We would like to hear from you. Please use the oposite side for
your comments.